Married to

HISTORICAL REGENCY ROMANCE NOVEL

Dorothy Sheldon

Copyright © 2025 by Dorothy Sheldon
All Rights Reserved.
This book may not be reproduced or transmitted in any form without the written permission of the publisher. In no way is it legal to reproduce, duplicate, or transmit any part of this document in either electronic means or in printed format. Recording of this publication is strictly prohibited and any storage of this document is not allowed unless with written permission from the publisher.

Table of Contents

Prologue 3
Chapter One 7
Chapter Two 15
Chapter Three 20
Chapter Four...28
Chapter Five..33
Chapter Six..40
Chapter Seven...48
Chapter Eight 53
Chapter Nine...58
Chapter Ten 64
Chapter Eleven 70
Chapter Twelve...74
Chapter Fourteen 85
Chapter Fifteen...89
Chapter Sixteen 96
Chapter Seventeen 103
Chapter Eighteen 106
Chapter Nineteen 112
Chapter Twenty 117
Chapter Twenty-One 123
Epilogue 126
Extended Epilogue 131

Prologue

"Whatever are you doing?" Rupert flung his head back and laughed aloud as his closest and dearest friend attempted to climb onto his horse. "You have been too much in the liquor for riding, Chesterton!"

"I think not." Lord Chesterton steadied himself as the horse stood stock still, perhaps sensing that his master was not entirely himself. "I am more than able, not only to ride but to shoot! I fully intend to join the hunt."

Rupert rolled his eyes and leaned one arm on the horse's stall. "I hardly think so."

"Yes, I shall!" Lord Chesterton, frowning hard, pulled himself up onto his horse and, much to Rupert's surprise, did not immediately slide off the other side. "Ah-hah!" Letting out a triumphant cry, he pushed himself to sit tall, grasping the pommel and holding on tightly. "You see? I am quite well."

With a small sigh, Rupert considered what he ought to do. Lord Chesterton was in high spirits for, only some three days ago, he had become engaged to the young lady he had been courting for the last month or so. Even better, he had become engaged at Rupert's house gathering which had made the occasion all the more delightful.

That being said, he did not think that Lord Chesterton joining the hunt was a wise idea. The small glass of brandy after luncheon had become another and then another as Lord Chesterton had spoken at length about what he was to face in married life, making Rupert wonder whether the gentleman was truly delighted at the prospect or if there was a little anxiety there, hidden underneath it all. Ought he to permit him to join the other guests for the hunt? If he fell from his horse, that could be dangerous indeed. And he certainly had no intention of offering Lord Chesterton a gun!

"You cannot prevent me, Wessex! I insist!"

"I am the Duke of Wessex, this is *my* house gathering and I can easily prevent you should I wish it," Rupert answered, firmly, as Lord Chesterton managed to turn his horse around so that it now faced the entrance of the stable. "It is not only my sister that I can command, my friend! I really do think that –"

"Please do not prevent me."

Rupert stopped, a little astonished to hear a sense of pleading begin to pervade Lord Chesterton's voice.

"I know I have imbibed a little too much but that does not matter, not to me." Lord Chesterton's hands were tight on the reins, looking at Rupert with a steadiness in his eyes that did not seem to match the slight slurring of his words. "I want to ride. I want to hunt. Pray, do not stop me."

"Chesterton." Rupert frowned, coming to stand a little closer to his friend, looking up at him. "Are you quite well?"

His friend's jaw went slack and he looked away. "I am well enough," he answered, without giving Rupert a real answer. "Are you going to let me participate?"

Chewing on the edge of his lip, Rupert held his friend's gaze. "I will let you ride but you cannot shoot," he said, firmly, even though Lord Chesterton let out a huff of breath and looked away. "I am doing my best for you, Chesterton, even though you might not think it." He was going to say more, to state that Lord Chesterton had been the one to choose the liquor but Rupert told himself not to. It would not bring him any relief and Lord Chesterton would remain frustrated.

"I shall tell Lady Dinah about you."

Rupert's lips quirked. "Indeed?" he remarked, his thoughts going at once to Lady Dinah, the daughter of the Marquess of Kent. For the last few months, he had taken note of her and now, at this house gathering, he had finally felt her close enough to propose. His intention was to do so very soon, something that only Lord Chesterton knew of. "And what shall you tell her?"

"That you are cruel and inconsiderate," Lord Chesterton said, heavily. "That you are much too demanding and authoritative and she ought not to accept your proposal."

Chuckling quietly and not taking a single thing Lord Chesterton had said to heart, Rupert gestured to the door. "Come now, my friend. Let us take our leave of the stables so I might begin the hunt. The other three gentlemen are already waiting."

"As is your horse," Lord Chesterton muttered, grumpily. "If you had told them to saddle mine when they saddled the others, then we would not have been tardy."

Rupert said nothing but watched his friend carefully as he rode out of the stable. Lord Chesterton was able to hold the reins securely and guide his horse out safely enough, though whether that was the horse knowing where to go rather than Lord Chesterton directing it, Rupert could not be sure. Running one hand over his chin, he followed out after Lord Chesterton, not at all sure that he had made the right decision. A knot of concern wove itself tightly into his stomach as he mounted his horse, glancing at his friend and seeing the way he scowled back at him.

"Are we ready?" he asked the other gentlemen, who all nodded and smiled at him, ready for their hunt. "Then let us go!"

***

The afternoon turned wet and cold by the time Rupert and his friends began to make their return from the hunt. They had enjoyed some shooting and had a few pheasants to show for it, though Lord Chesterton had grumbled and complained most fervently that he had no gun. Rupert did his best not to respond, hoping that, once Lord Chesterton recovered himself from his imbibing, he would appreciate Rupert's determinations. Sighing to himself, he turned his head, making sure that the other gentlemen were following after him, Lord Chesterton included, only to see Lord Chesterton holding one of their guns.

"Wait a moment!" he exclaimed, turning around as Lord Chesterton pulled his horse to the left, returning back the way they had come. "Chesterton, come now, you cannot do such a foolish thing!"

His friend did not deign to glance back at him. Instead, he rode back towards the trees, the horse cantering now and Lord Chesterton looking increasingly wobbly, making Rupert fear he might fall at any moment.

"We must go back with him," he said, gesturing for the other gentlemen to come after him. "Quite how he found a gun, I do not know!" The footmen who had accompanied them had been sent back to the house with all the guns and the like, for they would not be needing it any longer. Had Lord Chesterton waylaid one of them and taken a gun back? Why had Rupert not seen it? Frustrated, he squeezed his horse's sides and, with the other gentlemen riding ahead of him, pursued Lord Chesterton.

The trees were heavy with branches, the shadows going this way and that. They had already ridden through this dense forest on their way to the shoot and Rupert knew all too well they would find very little to hunt here! There were too many trees, to many places for the birds to hide which meant that Lord Chesterton could *only* be going in one direction – to the clearing that lead towards the open fields on the other side of the forest. This forest was well known to Rupert, the paths all laid out like a map in his head so he knew precisely where to go.

"You go ahead!" he called to the gentlemen in front of him. "He is making for the clearing, no doubt. I will go around and cut him off from the other side."

One of the other gentlemen nodded and nudged his horse a little faster though it was not as if they were all easily able to ride through the forest at great speed! Taking the path that broke to his right, Rupert made his way through the forest, his heart quickening as he pursued Lord Chesterton. Whatever was his friend thinking? It was one thing to be frustrated that he could not hunt but quite another to demand a gun and then ride off alone! Especially when he was in his cups! Gritting his teeth in frustration, Rupert urged the horse a little more quickly now, seeing the clearing up ahead.

And then, the most dreadful sound rent the air, stealing away his breath with a sudden sense of dread. Pulling the reins back sharply, the horse came to a stop and he, breathing heavily, stared straight ahead.

That had been a gunshot.

There was only one gun, he knew, one gun that Lord Chesterton had in his possession – but why would he shoot it now? Surely he had not made it to the clearing, dismounted, loaded his gun and thereafter, walked slowly and quietly so he might find something to take aim at? Squeezing his eyes closed, Rupert took in a long, calming breath, told himself silently that all would be well and began to ride again. The clearing soon came into view though, much to Rupert's surprise, the other gentlemen were already present. Had he really paused for so long?

"What has happened?" he asked, throwing himself down from his horse and coming to where the other gentlemen were standing, crowded around together. "I heard a shot and –"

His gasp was audible, one hand flying to his mouth as, eyes wide, he stared down at the prone figure of Lord Chesterton. There was blood on his breeches coming from a wound in his thigh and spilling out onto the grass beside him.

"I – I do not know what we ought to do," one of the gentlemen said, his face white as Rupert flung himself down beside his friend. "We are so far from the estate and..."

"He is breathing." Rupert closed his eyes for only a moment, taking that time to steady himself. *This is all my fault. I ought never to have permitted him to come.*

"I shall go to the house," another of the gentlemen said, getting back on his horse. "And send for the physician, mayhap?"

"Yes, do so." Pulling off his gloves, Rupert set one and then the other onto the wound before shrugging out of his jacket. Wrapping it around Lord Chesterton's leg as best he could, he kept looking to see if his friend would respond in any way, afraid that the pain would be too great... but Lord Chesterton's eyes remained closed, his face paler than ever. "Help me to lift him. I must get him back to the house as quickly as I can."

Within a few minutes, Lord Chesterton was half sitting, half lying on the horse with Rupert behind him. His horse was strong, Rupert knew, but all the same, they would not be able to make their way back to the house with any great speed. He did not dare think of what might become of his friend, did not dare let himself imagine what the outcome might be. Setting his thoughts solely on the manor house, Rupert kicked at his horse and began his journey.

Whether his friend would survive or not, he could not tell. All he knew was that the responsibility for this accident fell solely upon *his* shoulders.

Chapter One

Two years later

The wedding was over. That much was a relief, though Rupert knew there was still some more societal requirements to come. There was the wedding breakfast and, finally, the departure and that would be the end of it all.

He could hardly wait for that moment when the house would be his again, when it would have no-one but himself within it. Scowling, he made for his carriage, relieved that his duties were over. His sister was now the responsibility of the Marquess of Burnley and thus, he had nothing more to concern him.

Settling back in the carriage, Rupert closed his eyes and concentrated solely on his breathing, despising the weakness that had been in him before the wedding itself. He had been forced to deal with anxiety and that had repulsed him, hating that such a feebleness had been within him. When he had walked in with his sister Martha on his arm, he had felt every eye upon *him* rather than upon her, knowing full well that this unusual situation of him being present in company would have a good many of them talking about him once the day's events were at an end.

I do not want to be a part of them any longer, he reminded himself, a steely resistance to any sort of fine company returning to him again. *I am more than contented alone.*

The last two years had seen Rupert shrivel into himself, hiding away from anyone and everyone. The accident with Lord Chesterton had been so heavy upon him, it had spread guilt into every part of his being, breaking him with shame. Yes, his friend had not died but the injury to his leg had been severe and the broken arm – which had been discovered thereafter – had never properly healed, leaving him with a weakness that would always be with him. On top of that, Lord Chesterton's betrothal had been broken by the lady herself, leaving him desolate.

And it had all been Rupert's fault.

Once he had made sure Lord Chesterton was well on his way to recovery – as much of a recovery as could be had – Rupert had chosen to cloister himself at his estate. The guilt of his actions was so heavy, he had felt himself unable to step back into company again for fear of what would be said of him. All would know of his foolishness, of course, for the countryside around his estate had been rife with rumor and whisper. Nor could he bring himself to face society in the knowledge that *he* was responsible for Lord Chesterton's absence and his broken betrothal.

Rupert had never been sure how the accident had happened. Quite how Lord Chesterton had managed to discharge the gun so that it shot him in the leg, he could not understand but nor had he asked his friend for the details. It had not seemed right, for all that had mattered at that time had been whether or not Lord Chesterton would recover. The physician had worked quickly and effectively, given that Lord Chesterton still breathed, but the time for questions had never come to pass. Once Lord Chesterton was well enough to return home, he had done so – and Rupert had not spoken to him since. Lord Chesterton had written to him on two occasions thus far but Rupert had not been able to bring himself to open the letters, too afraid of what he would find within. Their friendship was at an end, *that* he understood which meant, as far as Rupert was concerned, he was unworthy of any sort of friendship ever again.

The carriage pulled into the driveway of his manor house and Rupert let out a slow breath, feeling frustration begin to tighten his limbs once more. He did not want to host the wedding breakfast but nor did he have a choice. This was the only thing that was left for him to do, he understood, but the thought of having guests return to his house made his stomach roil.

Getting out of the carriage without waiting for the footman to open the door, Rupert strode into his house and made his way directly to the study. The house was a hive of activity, with maids and servants carrying things this way and that, ready for the arrival of the guests. Rupert wanted nothing to do with it, eager to stay far from even his staff, if he could help it. Closing the door of his study behind him, he leaned against it and closed his eyes, breathing hard.

"Soon," he muttered to himself, opening his eyes and walking across the room to pour himself a small measure of whiskey. "Soon, I shall have my solitude again... and in a greater way than ever before."

At the beginning of the Season, he had sent his sister to London under the sharp, watchful eye of their mother, the Duchess of Wessex. That had brought him some relief, for no longer did he even have to sit with them over dinner and discuss inane matters. Nor would he have to hear his mother ask when *he* intended to marry, as though somehow it was perfectly feasible for him to make his way to London and choose a bride of his own.

Sighing heavily, he sat down in an overstuffed chair that faced the window, taking in the glorious sunshine that streamed through it.

He felt nothing.

Taking a sip of his whiskey, he let the heat flow through him and closed his eyes, leaning his head back against the chair in an attempt to quieten his mind and heart.

The door opened and he groaned.

"Did you forget that I was waiting?"

Rupert's eyes shot open and he turned his head. "Mother, you told me you were returning to the house with my sister."

"I did no such thing! *You* suggested that I might do such a thing and before I said yes or no, you disappeared into the church!" His mother, with her still dark hair and sharp blue eyes, put both hands to her hips. "That was not only disrespectful, it was inconsiderate."

"And unintended." Refusing to apologise, Rupert closed his eyes again. "Would you mind closing the door on your way out?"

"Out?"

Groaning loudly, Rupert cracked open one eye. "What is the matter now? Do you not have a daughter you can pay attention to?"

His mother's lips flattened.

"I do not need company. You know very well that I do not even *want* company."

"You shall have mine for a time, since Martha and Lord Kent have not yet arrived, though some of the other guests have made their way here already." Dropping her hands to her sides, the Duchess came to sit in the chair opposite, her gaze intense and steady, making Rupert's lip curl into a grimace.

"Mother, please. You know that I am finding this day somewhat trying."

"I care not. This day is not about you or your feelings," came the sharp reply. "It is about your sister and her happiness."

His lip curled all the more. "Which is why I am doing all that is required of me to make sure she has a happy day," he said, instantly defensive. "There can be no fault for you to find here, I am sure."

Something about what he had said softened his mother's expression, making Rupert frown. This gentleness was not what he wanted either, for that would lead to expressions of sympathy and thereafter, what he ought to do to change his present circumstances.

He did not want any of it.

"You must marry."

With a scowl, Rupert sat up straight, one hand curled into a tight fist. "What I need, Mother, is for you *not* to involve yourself in my life at present."

"Except I have to." Her eyes melded to his, her mouth an angry line as the softness he had seen faded. "You and I are to live in this house together until you wed and, truth be told, I have no interest in being here with you."

"Then go to the Dower house," Rupert answered, his fingernails biting into the soft skin of his palm. "Reside there, for all I care. "

"And bring yet more rumours to our family name?"

Those words bit down hard and Rupert flinched visibly.

"I do not say that to suggest you are in any way responsible," she continued, the firmness still in her tone and her gaze still fixed. "You know that I do not believe you were, though you continue to pull the cloak of guilt over your shoulders without hesitation."

Rupert gritted his teeth and looked away. "I do not want to speak of Lord Chesterton."

"Good, because we are not," came the quick reply. "We are talking of you and your need to marry. Or do you want this family line to fall to your uncle?"

This made Rupert's heart drop to the floor, fully aware of what his mother meant. His uncle was next in line and he was an utterly despicable fellow who was, at present, living in near poverty given just how much of his coin he wasted on gambling and the like. Rupert knew all too well that he had a responsibility to prove himself as the heir and whenever he thought of his uncle, that responsibility weighed on him all the heavier which was why, most of the time, he did all he could to forget about him.

"I have a solution."

"A solution?" Rupert repeated at once, his eyebrows lifting. "Mother, please do not tell me you have found some woebegone creature who is in desperate need of a marriage in order to save her family's honour – or their coffers – for I will *not*, under any circumstances, wed such a creature."

A glimmer of a smile brushed across his mother's face. "There is a Lady Marie who I should like to introduce to you. She is very dear friends with Martha and I am sure would suit you *very* well."

Rupert snorted, getting up to pour a second measure of whiskey, even though he knew he ought not to do so. Ever since Lord Chesterton's accident, he had barely imbibed at all and had silently promised himself he would never become drunk. "I hardly think that you know what would suit me, Mother."

"Oh, but I do." She held up one hand and began to tick her fingers off, one at a time. "You desire a young lady who is beautiful, do you not? One who would capture your attention. Thereafter, she must be considerate and, most of all, quiet." Her shoulders dropped a little. "She must do all she can to stay far from you and be content in her own company, even if it lasts for a long duration. Is that not so?"

Opening his mouth to deny all that his mother had said, Rupert was forced to close it again, seeing that she had said everything perfectly. Instead, he returned to his chair and slouched down into it, wishing desperately that his mother would bring this conversation to a close and she would return to his sister.

"Lady Marie would do you well," she continued, when he said nothing. "She is very contented in her own company, she is quite lovely in her own way and I am all too aware of just how much her father desires her to marry."

"Then why is she not wed?" Rupert asked, frowning but surprised that he was not instantly refusing to even think on such an idea. "You said she was in London with Martha. What is it about her that had no gentlemen pursuing her?"

His mother lifted her shoulders and let them fall. "I cannot imagine."

Studying his mother's face carefully, Rupert tried to ascertain if there was something more behind all that she said but he could not. The Duchess was simply looking back at him with a clear expression, waiting for him to respond.

"I do not need your help when it comes to matrimony," Rupert stated, after a short silence. "When the time comes, I will choose my own bride and I shall marry."

His mother shook her head. "When the time comes?" she asked, as she rose to her feet. "You have not moved from this house in two years and, instead of seeing any sort of positive, contented and happy change within you, it is clear to me that there is nothing but sadness and regret. Why will you not think about it? To dismiss it at once is foolish."

Because I do not want to marry.

Rupert dropped his head into one hand, his fingers pushing through his dark hair as a long breath of exasperation left him.

But I have to.

That was true enough, at least. He could not escape that fact and even though he wanted to push it aside, to pretend that it did not matter, he could not.

"Will you at least let me introduce you to her?" His mother inched forward in her seat, her eyes searching his face but Rupert let out a breath and looked away, angry that she had been so easily able to twist his thoughts with her words. The only reason he was thinking about marriage, the only reason he was considering what she had said was because of the mention of his uncle and the hinted suggestion that he was not doing as he ought as regarded his responsibilities.

"There is no need." Rupert lifted his chin and kept his gaze steady. "I have no need for you, my mother, to find me a suitable match. I am well able to do that on my own."

Her eyes narrowed. "In what way?" she asked, a hint of anger in the way her lips thinned. "How are *you* to find a match when you have not moved from this estate in two years?"

Rupert could give her no answer.

"Think on this, my son," she said, refusing to look away from him but holding him with the intensity of her gaze. "If you stay where you are, if you continue to linger at this estate, then it shall be you and I residing here together." The corner of her mouth lifted for only a moment and Rupert's stomach dropped, feeling as though he were about to be caught in a snare of her making. "Do not think that I shall be happy and contented to linger here alone with you," she continued, her voice quieter now but her words holding a good deal more weight. "I shall have to have many a friend present. Indeed, I may have a soiree now and again, or perhaps a house ball of my own."

The very thing that Rupert despised was pushed towards him, a path that he would be forced to walk upon.

"You know you cannot refuse me such things, given that I reside here also at present," his mother continued. "This solitude that you so desperately desire will evade you, my son... though to my mind, that is no bad thing given that you are so determined to cling to it despite the fact that it causes you nothing but further pain."

"You can remove to the Dower house," Rupert said, repeating the suggestion from earlier in the conversation. "We have already discussed that and I told you –"

His mother held up one hand, palm out. "I shall do nothing of the sort," she said, clearly. "Until you are wed, my place is here. Therefore, until you wed, I shall be under this roof and in this home." Her head tilted. "Unless it is that you have secret intentions of making your way to London and finding a bride there? That would surprise me, certainly but it would not displease me."

A low growl from Rupert's chest was her only answer.

"Then I propose that you introduce yourself to Lady Marie and consider her as a potential bride," his mother said, not in the least bit perturbed by his harsh response. "Why should you refuse me? This idea is an excellent one, for you can marry a lady that will give you all the solitude that you desire *and* can provide the required heir. Think on it, Wessex! This house could be split in two, so that she resides in one part and you in the other."

"*You* could do such a thing," Rupert muttered, looking away from her and finding his heart trembling within his chest. "*You* could reside separately from me, if you chose to do so."

The laugh that broke from her lips did nothing but antagonize Rupert all the more and he threw back the rest of his whiskey in an attempt to calm his anger.

It only added fuel to it.

"My dear son, need I remind you that I have lived in this house for many a year more than you?"

"You do not need to remind me, Mother."

"Then what right have you to make such a suggestion?"

Rupert's anger broke apart in a moment as tears glimmered in his mother's eyes. She got to her feet, one hand pointing out towards him.

"When did you think it right to speak to me with such disrespect? When did your character of kindness and consideration change into this dark, shadowed creature you are now?"

His mouth went dry, no answer coming to his lips. She was quite right, he knew. He ought never to have suggested such a thing. Indeed, it had come from a place of irritation and upset but he had not set a guard on his words as he ought to have done.

"Your father brought me here on our wedding day." A single tear slipped down her cheek. "Now, so many years later, I have my very own son suggesting that I hide myself away from his company so that *he* can be more comfortable?"

Dropping his head forward, Rupert said nothing, shame burning in his chest.

"Can you not see that, even in this, I am doing my utmost to care for you as a mother ought?" Her voice had lost none of its strength but he could hear the slight quaver in her words. "You turn me away at every point, choosing darkness instead of permitting even a single flicker of light to break through to you."

Rupert closed his eyes. "You have said quite enough. Please, will you not now return to Martha? You are wasted on me, Mother."

He did not open them again until he heard the rustle of her skirts and her footsteps leading her away from him. Out of the corner of his eye, he saw her open the door and, giving him a long look, she stepped out into the hallway.

Relief floored him and he closed his eyes again, going almost entirely limp as he sank back into the chair. The last thing he wanted to talk about, to *think* about was matrimony and yet, here his mother was attempting to force him to do so. The idea of sharing this house with a bride was unthinkable, for he would never again have his solitude!

Though you are never to have it here either.

His eyes opened, a scowl pulling at his mouth.

Your mother has as much right to do as she pleases in this house. Coming thick and fast, his thoughts crowded him, making his brow furrow. *She will do just as she has said, for she does not crave the same isolation as I.*

How was he to free himself from this, then? If his mother was always to be present, always to be with him until he wed, then he would never gain the seclusion he so desperately desired.

Unless...

Scrubbing one hand over his eyes, Rupert tried not to let his thoughts turn to what his mother had said, determining silently that this was nothing more than foolishness but, the more he did so, the more they pushed into his mind.

What if there was a way in which he *could* have his isolation and be wed at the same time? His mother could not be given a particular set of rooms to keep to given that she had lived here for most of her years but a wife... well, that was different, was it not? His mother's suggestion had not been a poor one, then, he realized. It could be that his bride was told precisely what it was he expected and that, in knowing that, would do just as he had stated. He would not need to be in her company for very long at all, only present to do the required duties and nothing more.

And what of Lady Marie?

Rupert grimaced, getting to his feet to get yet another measure of whiskey. He did not want to give in, did not want to do as his mother had suggested and permit her to introduce him to this young lady but that came from his own pride, he recognized. Besides which, how exactly was he to find a suitable match? Did he really think that he could make his way to London, step into society and find himself flocked by eager young ladies all desiring to know him better? His stomach turned over at that thought, leaving him with a resolve not to do so. The chances were that, even if he *did* go to London, the whispers about him and the shame that would follow would be too much to bear.

Which meant he had only one choice.

The only difficulty was, he simply did not want to accept it.

Chapter Two

"You are so *very* kind, Martha." Marie grasped her friend's hand, beaming at her. "To have invited me to your wedding when we have only been friends for a few months is generosity indeed."

"Oh, but of course!" Lady Martha – now Lady Kent – squeezed Marie's hand. "Our friendship has been such a blessing to me, I assure you. When I first came to London, I was quite certain I would not find a single soul willing to befriend me! But you proved to me that my concerns were nothing but dust and ashes, ready to be blown away."

Marie smiled back at her friend, aware that what Martha spoke of, she did not fully understand. It was quite true that Martha had held some deep concerns over what the *ton* might think of her but Marie had never truly understood why. Martha was the sister of a Duke which meant her connections were very strong indeed and her standing almost the highest in all of England! All the same, she had encouraged Martha where she could and they had ended up becoming very close friends though Marie had never once questioned her as to where such concerns came from. She had thought to herself that if Martha had wanted to explain, then she would have done and thus, no clarification had come.

"And now I am wed!" Martha released Marie's hand and sighed contentedly, a dazzling smile on her face. "Lord Kent is the most wonderful gentleman and I am sure I shall be very happy with him."

"I am certain you will," Marie answered, turning her head to see Lord Kent laughing loudly at something another had said, though she did not miss the way he glanced towards his bride. Her heart squeezed, both with happiness for her friend and a hint of jealousy though she did her best to quash the latter. "As for myself, I must continue on in the hope of finding a suitable gentleman." She winced as she saw Martha's sympathetic smile. "You know as well as I that my father now despairs of me utterly. He is quite sure that I shall end up a spinster and that, to his mind, is nothing more than a shame upon the family."

"I cannot imagine that you will have no husband at all," Martha answered, stoutly. "You need to find a gentleman who is just as Lord Kent is to me – considerate, accepting and generous. There are bound to be many gentlemen like that in England, I am sure!"

Her friend's encouragements made Marie smile, though her hopes did not lift with the curve of her lips. "Let us hope you are right, though I suspect that very few gentlemen want a bluestocking for a bride! And as I have said to my father, whether I hide it now or not, they will discover the truth about me eventually – and I will not be content with being despised by my husband."

"I think that is very wise," her friend replied, though her gaze soon returned to Lord Kent rather than looking at Marie. "One must be respected and considered by one's husband, I quite agree. That is the key to a happy and contented marriage, I am quite sure. Lord Kent knows everything about me and I am sure I know near enough everything about him!" Her nose wrinkled, her attention returning to Marie. "There are some things that I do not like, of course, but I would never think lesser of him because of it."

"Oh?" Marie was a little surprised to hear this for she had never heard her friend say anything untoward about Lord Kent before.

"He does not approve of my brother," Martha answered, with a small but sad smile. "I have not told you of this, I know, but I did not want you to think poorly of him."

"Of your brother?"

"Of Lord Kent," Martha answered, with a wry tug of her lips. "I have not told you a good deal about my brother, I know, but that is for good reason. And indeed, the less I say about him, the better for it is of no importance to you whether you know him or not. Indeed, I might go as far as to say that not to be introduced to him is a good thing!"

Wondering if the champagne that Martha had drunk was now loosening her lips a little, Marie hesitated, aware that she wanted to pry a little more but that the only reason she would do so was to satisfy her own curiosity. "I am not sure I shall be able to remain unacquainted," she said, after a few moments of silence. "We are at your wedding breakfast after all, which is being held in his manor house!"

This made Martha grimace, astonishing Marie all the more. Did she truly think so little of her brother? Or was there something more to her dislike?

"He may well hide himself away in his study and refuse to come out until it is time for Lord Kent and I to take our leave." With a heavy sigh, Martha turned her head towards Lord Kent and then looked back at Marie. "Lord Kent thinks my brother foolish in his decision to stay far from the *ton* and hide himself away at this estate. Nor did he think it right for him to send my mother and I to London for the Season without attending himself, for I am his only sister and Lord Kent felt it would be the right thing for him to do."

Marie said nothing, reaching to take a glass of champagne from a passing footman's tray though she listened keenly as Martha continued, getting the sense that her friend was unburdening herself somewhat.

"I did so very much want my brother to attend my come out and I told him of my desire, but he was determined to do just as he pleased, despite my desire."

"That is a pity," Marie murmured, not quite sure what else she ought to say. "I am sure he had his reasons for remaining."

Martha laughed but it was not a happy sound. "Oh, I am sure that he did but they were all selfish reasons, were they not? Ever since that house gathering, he has thought of no one but himself, becoming frustrated, at times, with even the smallest conversation!"

"House gathering?"

Martha waved one hand vaguely. "It was some two years ago and something happened – something that was not his fault but he has taken it as his own. Because of that, he has become near enough a recluse and that, mayhap, I would not mind so much if it was his own choice but he has become so cruel with it all that it is deeply upsetting to both myself and my mother." A heavy breath escaped her, quite at odds with the joy that filled the rest of the day. "I am a little concerned about leaving my mother here with him, truth be told. I am to be happily married, indeed, but what of her? Is she to reside here with him alone? I do not know what that will do to her!"

"I am sure your mother will do very well," Marie answered, not at all sure as to what she was speaking into but feeling the need to reassure her friend all the same. "She is a strong willed lady, is she not? She was well able to look after you during the Season, yes? She navigated that very well I thought. You do not need to worry, I am certain." When Martha's expression did not alter from one of concern, Marie filled her voice with enthusiasm. "Besides which, are you not able to invite her to reside with you for a time? She will be delighted at such an invitation, I am sure!"

This, much to Marie's relief, brought a smile back to Martha's face. "Indeed, I could! Lord Kent has already said as much. Thank you, Marie, I had quite forgotten that." A contented sigh left her lips as she smiled. "I shall be able to invite her to reside with us once the honeymoon is over. That means she will not have to endure him for long."

"Endure? Who shall have to endure?"

The smiling face of the Duchess of Wessex came to join them, breaking into the conversation though neither Marie nor Martha answered her. The Duchess, lifting an eyebrow, looked from one to the other, a curious smile on her face. "I do hope you are not speaking of marriage; else I have made a great mistake in permitting you to wed Lord Kent!"

At this, Martha laughed and shook her head, leaning into her mother for a moment. "No, not in the least. I was speaking of something else."

"I see." The Duchess did not question this, making to say something more, only for her eyes to round as her gaze went over Marie's shoulder. Marie, noticing this, fought the urge to look around, wondering what it was that had caught the Duchess' attention so.

"Here you are, then."

A low, dark voice made Marie shiver but still, she did not move, aware of the prickling of her skin.

"I have thought about your suggestion," the gentleman said, slowly. "I shall be introduced but that is all."

"Being introduced to new acquaintances is a *marvelous* way to gain a few more friendships!" the Duchess interrupted, her voice a trifle louder than before and a slightly panicked look on her face, though Marie did not understand why she should appear so. "Might I begin by introducing Lady Marie to you?"

The gentleman came a little further around and Marie looked up into his face, only for her heart to plummet to the floor. This gentleman did not appear to be in the least bit pleased to be introduced to her. A grimace pulled at his lips, his nose wrinkling just a little. Dark hair was flung over his forehead, his eyebrows low and heavy over shadowed blue eyes. His jaw was set tight, his gaze assessing rather than inviting.

She shivered.

"Might I introduce my son to you, Lady Marie?" The Duchess smiled warmly at Marie, the very opposite of what this gentleman was doing. "This is the Duke of Wessex. Wessex, this is Lady Marie, daughter to the Earl of Stockbridge."

Marie did her best to smile as she dropped into a curtsy. "A pleasure to meet you, Your Grace."

"Hmph." The Duke did not so much as bow, making Marie's heart quail all the more. Was there something wrong with her? Something that had upset him? "Well, the introduction is done now, is it not?" He looked to his mother, one eyebrow lifted slightly. "I shall take my leave of you now."

"I –"

The response died on the Duchess' lips as the Duke walked away from them all, his shoulders pulled back and his head held high. He did not stop to speak to any other but instead made his way directly through the growing crowd and seated himself at the extremity of the room as if he did not want to speak to a single soul.

"My apologies." The Dowager Duchess put one hand to her heart and gave Marie a rueful smile. "I am afraid that my son is a little overwhelmed with his duties at the present moment and is not thinking about propriety."

"Or good manners," Martha put in, taking Marie's hand and pressing it gently. "You are not to blame for his rudeness. Recall all that I have said to you before."

Marie nodded slowly, seeing the sharp look that the Duchess sent in Martha's direction though Martha appeared to ignore it entirely. "Of course," she said, managing to set aside her embarrassment and smile instead. "You are quite right. He will have his duties sitting upon his mind, I am sure and will find himself distracted. Pray, do not be concerned. I am not at all upset."

Visible relief pooled into the Duchess' eyes as a heavy breath escaped her. "That is good. I thank you for your understanding, Lady Marie. Now, if you will excuse me, I must see if the dining table is prepared for us all. And Martha," she finished, directing her final few words to her daughter, "*you* must go to stand beside your husband, ready to lead everyone into the room."

Martha beamed at her mother, cheeks flushing pink as the thought of being side by side with her husband pushed away all previous concern. "But of course, Mama," she said, pressing Marie's hand again and then stepping away. "I shall speak to you again, Marie, very soon."

With a nod and a smile, Marie watched her friend make her way back towards her husband, seeing how delighted Lord Kent appeared to be at her arrival. He not only took her hand but pressed a kiss to it; a most unexpected expression of affection though given that it was their wedding day, Marie assumed most of the guests would expect it instead of exclaiming over it! As she took a sip of her champagne, Marie let her gaze rove over the guests. There were many of them and they all appeared to be laughing or smiling in clear enjoyment of the occasion, all save one. A light shiver ran through her as she looked straight back into the Duke's eyes. Even from a distance, he was able to set a tremble across her skin and she quickly pulled her gaze away.

Now, having met him, she could well understand why Martha had not spoken of him in detail. He was, to her mind, somewhat terrifying given his dark looks and ill manner! Little wonder that he wanted to be at this house alone, for Marie was quite sure he would not easily find company willing to put up with such somberness!

But I shall not think of that now, she told herself, firmly. *I am here to congratulate Martha on her wedding and enjoy the wedding breakfast and that is precisely what I shall do.*

Chapter Three

Rupert looked at his reflection in the mirror, taking in the shadows under his eyes, the set of his jaw and the weight in his shoulders. The wedding had been a sennight ago and still, he felt the effects of it upon him. Of course, the guests were gone and the house had been restored to order but still, he could not find a sense of peace within him.

It is all because of her.

Scowling at his reflection, Rupert turned on his heel and strode from the room. He spoke to no-one, the footmen stepping respectfully out of his path or melting into the shadows as though they knew of his desire to be entirely alone. Making his way directly to his study, as he did almost every day, Rupert shut the door tightly and, still scowling, marched to the window and gazed out.

His mother, as he had expected, was taking tea in the gardens, sitting in the arbor so that she was shaded from the rays of the sun. She sat there every morning when it was warm though retreated indoors if it rained. This time, however, she did not appear to be alone.

Rupert's stomach flipped over. When had she informed him that she was to have guests? It was not exactly early in the day but all the same, he would have expected her to have told him if she was to have company.

Not that it would make much difference, he reminded himself, turning away from the window. *I intend to remain in here or in the library for the day regardless.*

This was how he spent his days now. The last two years, he had spent as much time in his own company as he could, feeling himself retreat from even his own mother and sister. Their conversation frustrated him, the inane things they spoke of angering him. He did not care which lady had married which gentleman, did not care about the Season or anything to do with society. He was no longer a part of it and, therefore, wanted very little to do with it all.

And yet, they had always insisted on speaking of whatever they pleased without consideration for him.

Just as mother insists on doing now.

Rubbing one hand over his face, Rupert sat down heavily in his chair and pulled out his accounts. This morning, he was to look over all of the outgoings from the previous few months to make sure all was well. Trying to concentrate on the numbers, he found his jaw tightening when a peal of laughter rose up from the gardens to his window. He wanted silence, did he not? He *demanded* silence and yet his mother insisted on ignoring such a demand! How was he meant to concentrate when she made such noise?

Pushing the accounts to one side, he picked up his correspondence, noting that it was only three letters. A small frown dug into his forehead, recalling when he had once received multiple letters each day – not only on business matters but also from friends and acquaintances, eager to know when they would next be in his company.

"That was before I did such a ridiculous thing that almost claimed the life of my friend," he reminded himself aloud, the shame of it springing back into his mind and settling on his heart all over again. "Before I showed myself to be nothing but a simpleton."

The darkness came on him heavily again, just as it always did. It did not matter whether he rose early or late in the day, at some point it would return to cloud his mind and settle itself around him like a cloak that he could not throw aside. It was expected now; a regular part of his day that he could never seem to escape from... and mayhap did not even want to. It was his experience, his daily experience and, even though he knew it had not always been so, it felt as if he had always carried it.

The first letter was naught but business affairs, with his man of business in London informing him that his holdings on the continent were doing well and that he intended to make his journey there within the next sennight, as had been arranged. Rupert discarded that, for there was no need for him to respond to it and picked up the second.

This softened his heart a little, for the sweetness of his sister's gratitude for all he had done for her on her wedding day was most welcome. In his heart, Rupert felt a sense of guilt over how unbrotherly he had been towards her these last two years, recalling the day she had begged him to come to London with her so she might make her come out properly... and the day he had driven her to tears by his refusal.

"She did not understand," he told himself aloud, in an attempt to take some of the guilt from himself. "She could not. Not truly."

It does not matter now anyway, he told himself, setting the letter down. *She is happily married and that was the whole point of her going to London anyway.*

Picking up the third, he paused, looking down at the seal and struggling to recognize it. He always checked the seals carefully, for if any came from Lord Chesterton, he set them to one side, unable to bring himself to open them for fear of what would be contained within. That made him angry with his own weakness all the more but, despite that, he could not bring himself to do anything other than that.

Breaking the seal, he unfolded the letter and laid it out. Rather than looking at the beginning, he dropped his gaze to the end.

Lord Stockbridge.

The name seemed familiar to him but Rupert could not place it. Beginning to read, his eyebrows lifted higher and higher in astonishment, swiftly replaced by a growing frustration.

'Your Grace, first might I thank you for the time given to the reading of this letter since, as yet, we have not been introduced. It was my youngest daughter, Lady Marie, who was in attendance at your estate lately, along with her mother who accompanied her as her chaperone. I understand that you were introduced to Marie and she has spoken very well of the interaction between you.'

Rupert rolled his eyes at this, quite sure that the lady had said nothing of the sort. He knew as well as she that he had spoken sharply, that he had responded to the interaction in a rude and improper manner before walking away from her directly. That was certainly not something to speak well of!

'Marie is the youngest of my daughters and the only one unwed,' the letter continued, making Rupert's eyebrows fall and knot together. 'My wife spoke at length to the Duchess of Wessex and I hear that a suggested match was discussed. I am writing to you in the hope that you yourself were interested in the proposal, though if you were not, then I quite understand. I have found it very difficult indeed to have any gentleman take note of Marie for, despite her beauty, she is determined to be a bluestocking no matter what is said of her! It is a faint hope I have only and I fully understand if this is not a matter you would wish to discuss any further. However, if there is even the smallest of interest, then might we meet to talk the matter over? There would be no obligation, even then, but I should be glad to tell you as much about Marie as you might wish. The Duchess made it clear that we were welcome to come to call whenever we might wish, though I should not wish to trespass on your generosity too often, Your Grace.'

The letter ended with various accolades and the like but Rupert did not even read them all, such was his irritation. His mother had, it seemed, spoken with Lady Marie's mother without even mentioning it to him! She had made the suggestion of the match in the full awareness that he had not consented to it! Why had she thought to do such a thing? Was she truly so determined to force this match upon him?

His fingers gripped the letter tightly, the urge to crumple it up and throw it into the fireplace -ready to be burned- fighting through him. Instead, pushing himself out of his chair, he stormed to the door and threw it open. Striding to the front of the house, he made his way outside and directly towards his mother, heedless to who else was present.

"You spoke to Lady Stockbridge?" Barely throwing a glance to the visitor, Rupert brandished the letter in front of his mother's face. "You suggested that –"

"Wessex!" His mother rose directly, her face flaming but her eyes holding a sadness that Rupert could not help but respond to. "If you have something you wish to discuss with me, then might I suggest we do so in private?"

"I shall take my leave!" A lady that Rupert did not recognize got to her feet, her eyes darting to his and then pulling away again, a paleness in her cheeks that betrayed her concern over his presence there. "Luncheon did sound lovely but —"

"No, Eugenia, wait a moment, if you please." The Duchess gestured to her friend to sit back down, her voice quieter. "My son is being most improper and I can only apologise for his lack of consideration. If you will remain, I shall speak to him in the house and will return to you thereafter."

She did not give Rupert a chance to respond but quickly walked away from him and from her friend, her head held high with that familiar sense of quiet dignity surrounding her.

Shame was all that Rupert wore. The anger, which had thrown itself at him so quickly began to fade just as fast, leaving him with the overwhelming awareness that he ought not to have done such a thing. He should never have spoken to her as he did, should never have come out to where she sat with a friend and demanded his answers.

He closed his eyes, then turned on his heel to follow after his mother. Not a word of apology escaped his lips, however. His mother could apologise for him if she wished but he had no reason to give it to anyone.

"I am utterly ashamed of you."

The moment Rupert stepped into the house, his mother rounded on him, her eyes like shards of glass, tearing into him.

"How *dare* you speak to me in such a manner? Have you lost your senses? I am your mother and the Duchess of Wessex still! You have no right to throw yourself headlong into my conversation and expect to force answers from me!"

Rupert, crawling into his shame, dropped his gaze to the floor though still, he did not let himself speak an apology. Over the last two years, he had closed that part of himself off from anyone else, hiding his shame and upset from everyone. To apologise would show them that weakness and he had no intention of doing such a thing.

He was enough of a coward already.

"In answer to your question, yes, I *did* speak to Lady Stockbridge but it was not with the assumption that the match would go ahead!" she continued, blinking furiously now though Rupert could not tell whether the tears in her eyes were from upset or anger. "I wanted to make certain that the lady was, herself, free. If she was already courting, then there would be no discussion, would there?"

"You should have spoken to me about this first!" Rupert exclaimed, throwing up his hands, one still clutching the letter. "You should have asked me about the idea and —"

"Oh, but I did!" Putting both hands to her hips, his mother glared back at him. "I spoke with you, I suggested that you be introduced to the lady and thereafter, that is precisely what you did – though a very poor impression you made upon her, I am sure!"

Rupert opened his mouth to throw something back at her but instead, chose to stay silent rather than respond. He told himself that it was because he did not want to get into a furious argument with his mother which, no doubt, all of the staff could hear but if he was to be truthful with himself, Rupert knew it was only because he could not give her a clear answer. Indeed, he realized, she *had* come to speak with him about the possible match and certainly, she *had* suggested an introduction be the only thing he considered. And had he not done as she had said? Had he not gone for an introduction?

"You will be glad to know that the lady is, as yet, still unwed and not courting," his mother continued, when Rupert did not respond. "There is nothing that should hold you back from her now."

"Ah, but there is a reason she is unwed," Rupert answered, still angry with the way that his mother had gone about things. "She is a bluestocking! A *bluestocking,* Mother! Is that someone you truly wish for this family to be associated with? Imagine the rumours that would follow!"

The Duchess did not immediately respond. Her eyes searched his, softening now as though she recognized the darkness that was within his mind and wanted, somehow, to send a shard of light straight through it.

"Do you not think that there are rumours aplenty already?"

The question exploded in Rupert's mind and he looked away, his heart shattering with the response. Yes, he was all too aware that he had brought about plenty of rumors from the *ton* by his actions – and inaction thereafter – but he had never expected his mother to state such a thing outright.

"What would another rumour be?" she said, just as gently but the words still tore into his heart. "Why should you care what is said of you? Of this family?"

Lifting his head, Rupert looked dully back into his mother's eyes, wishing that he could find an answer to give her that would make sense, one that would push her away from him and leave him alone.

"All that matters to you – and to me, truth be told – is that the family line continues and the Dukedom does not pass to your uncle." The Duchess stepped forward and put a hand on his arm, though the touch brought Rupert no relief. "What is wrong with Lady Marie, aside from her love of reading and learning? I can think of nothing."

"I – I do not want to marry." The truth burned his lips but the words were spoken nonetheless, leaving his heart heavy as he dropped his head so he would not have to look at his mother. Her sympathy was more than he could bear, especially after how poorly he had behaved towards her.

"Whether you want to or not is besides the point," came the steady answer. "I will not force your hand for that is not my place nor my intention. But I beg of you, Rupert, consider the lady. She might be all that you require."

It was the first time in a long time that she had referred to him as 'Rupert'. When he had first been called 'the Duke of Wessex', Rupert had seen how difficult a change that had been for her, given that she had always called his father by that name. Over the last few years, that had become easier, until speaking to him as 'Wessex' had become familiar. To be called Rupert was to break his heart into tiny little smithereens, to make him feel as though he were a child again.

He hung his head.

"I will think on it." He had to force the words out, had to grate out every single syllable. He did not want to say such a thing, did not want to agree to it but all that she had said made sense.

"You could make everything very clear to her," his mother continued, still speaking with just as much gentleness as she had when she had spoken his name. "You could have the house arranged to your preference, could make sure she knows what your intentions are for your married life."

Rupert's lips flattened. "You want this very much, Mother, I know."

"I could move to the Dower house as well," she continued, as though she had not heard him. "You would be wed, a child would soon be on the way and given that she is a bluestocking... well, is that not all the better?"

A lift of his eyebrow was his only response.

"Because she will want to surround herself with books!" she exclaimed, as though he were foolish not to understand what she meant. "Your library is prolific and she will, I am sure, want very little to do with you when she sees just how much knowledge there is to be found within your library."

Something shifted in Rupert's being as he listened to his mother speak. Perhaps, indeed, this might be exactly what it was he needed. If he married Lady Marie, making it clear what their life together would be like, then what concern would he have? Yes, he would make sure a child was soon on the way but there was no need for him to spend any time with her, was there? And if it was as Lord Stockbridge had said, if she truly was a bluestocking who cared very little for what society thought of her, then that might be all the better! She could surround herself with books, might be able to have acquaintances nearby whom she could go to visit – for he would make it clear there were to be no guests here – and thus, he could have as much solitude as he pleased whilst fulfilling his duties at the very same time.

"Very well." Seeing the light jump into his mother's eyes, Rupert looked away, unsmiling. "I shall write to Lord Stockbridge and ask him to come to call. Their estate is not so very far away."

"A day's ride." His mother stepped back, her eyes still alight but searching his face as if she were afraid he would renege on his decision. "You shall need to have him remain."

Rupert scowled, wanting to do the very opposite of that but he realised that he had no choice.

"Will you write to him today?"

"Yes, I shall." Wearied by the conversation, Rupert turned away, making for his study. "Go back to your friend, Mother. I will have this letter written and sent away by the time your luncheon is finished."

His steps were heavy as he returned to his study, the fury that had blown through him on his way out to his mother now nothing but smoke. With a furrowed brow, he sat down at his desk again and looked at the letter from Lord Stockbridge, wondering if he was doing the right thing by responding in a positive manner to the gentleman.

"It is not as though I am accepting and going ahead with the marriage," he told himself aloud, pulling out a fresh piece of parchment. "This is only a discussion. Nothing more."

All that being said and the determination still in his mind, it took Rupert a few minutes more to put ink to paper. The words were few but to the point, telling the gentleman that he would be willing to discuss the proposal at his earliest convenience and, with irritation biting at him, that the gentleman would be welcome to come to stay overnight so they could talk at length.

That done, he sealed the letter and rose to his feet, ringing the bell for the footman to come. His feet began to take him from one end of the room to the other, pacing up and down as he waited, his irritation rising.

"Your Grace?"

Rupert turned sharply, ready to berate the footman for being tardy but found his tongue sticking to the roof of his mouth – and his hand gripping his letter tightly.

"I apologise, I thought that you rang the bell." The footman bowed and then made to step out of the room. "I shall go to resume my duties."

"Wait." Rupert scrubbed one hand over his face, aware of the reluctance within him to do what needed to be done. "I have a letter."

The footman glanced at Rupert's hand. "Yes, Your Grace." Coming a little closer to him, he held out one hand. "I shall have it sent away at once."

Making to lift his hand and give the letter to the footman, Rupert found himself stuck in position. His arm would not lift from his side, his hand would not reach out and give the letter to the waiting footman. Was it fear that kept him here? Or mere reluctance?

I am not afraid of matrimony, he told himself, seeing the flickering frown on the footman's face. *I cannot permit myself to let it hold me back.*

For a moment, his future rose up in front of him, a great, yawning unknown that threatened to swallow him whole. He knew what he wanted – isolation from all others so that he need not face the shame he bore nor ever be permitted to make such a mistake again – but despite his mother's assurance, what if this did not bring him all he desired? What if, instead, it was a trap ready to ensnare him?

"Your Grace?" The footman sounded hesitant. "Is that the letter or am I to fetch it from your desk?"

Enough!

Angry with his own feebleness, Rupert finally managed to thrust the letter at the astonished footman. "Take it at once." He watched as the footman scurried from the room, resisting the desire to shout him back, take the letter and rip it into pieces. The door closed and Rupert shut his eyes, swaying just a little as worry poured into his mind, threatening to overwhelm him.

It is done, he told himself, opening his eyes and going to pour a measure of brandy. *Now all I can do is wait.*

Chapter Four

"Marie?"

Hiding herself away, book in hand, Marie barely heard her mother calling her. She was so engrossed in what she was reading – a book on the varieties of birds found in France – that she only listened with half an ear. The arbor was quiet, hiding her from any watchful eyes and the birdsong around her was a beautiful and appropriate accompaniment to what she was reading.

"Marie!" Her mother's sharp exclamation made Marie flinch, nearly dropping the book as she turned her head to look up at her. How had she found her so quickly?

"Yes, Mama?"

"I have been calling you for almost half an hour! And none of the maids knew where you had gone."

Marie was about to state that the reason she was hiding herself away in the arbor was solely because she did not *want* to be found, only to think better of it given her mother's increasingly dark expression.

"It is only because one of the gardener's saw you skulking away over here that I knew where you had gone," her mother continued, her hands to her hips now. "Why must you hide so?"

"Because I want to read."

At this, Lady Stockbridge threw up her hands, her eyes rolling for only a moment. "That is all you ever wish to do, my dear! How are we ever going to have you married if you do nothing but have your focus solely on the words on a page!"

Marie swallowed hard and set the book down. Her father had never pushed her to wed, telling her that she would find the right gentleman when the time came and, much to her joy, encouraging her in her reading and her study. Her mother had been the same, though mayhap that had been more because she had focused all of her attentions upon Marie's siblings – all of whom were now wed and settled. She, being the youngest, had been the last to enter society.

Though, Marie considered, ever since Lady Martha had married, her mother had appeared to be a good deal more set on the notion of Marie marrying and marrying quickly. Indeed, they had gone to London for the Season and indeed, her mother had encouraged her as any mother ought, but initially, at least, it had not been as severe as Marie had expected. She had thought that her mother would be chiding her severely for her reading and her lack of interest in attending balls and the like, but Lady Stockbridge had reacted with seeming understanding and gentleness. However, after Lady Martha had made her betrothal, Marie observed that her mother's spirits seemed somewhat more enlivened.

Mayhap she had underestimated just how much of an impact Lady Martha's marriage had made.

"What is it you wanted to say, Mama?" Marie forced a smile she did not truly feel in the hope of placating her mother. "Is there anything I can help you with?"

"It is about your father," Lady Stockbridge said, coming into the arbor and sitting opposite Marie. "He did tell me that I ought not to tell you of his visit in case nothing comes of it but I strongly disagree with him in that and therefore, I have come to tell you the reason for your father's absence from the house."

Marie, sensing a storm beginning to swirl, clasped her hands tightly in her lap and held her mother's gaze. What was it that she was going to say?

"As you know, your dear friend, Lady Martha, was married to Lord Kent," Lady Stockbridge went on, when Marie did not say a word. "That wedding was very lovely, was it not?" Her expression softened for a moment and Marie, unable to help herself, smiled.

"Indeed, it was. Made all the more so by the affection shared between them."

This made her mother frown, hard. "Affection is not something that you will need to pursue in marriage," she said, much too firmly for Marie's liking. "It may come, yes and it is certainly a delightful thing when one can have it but it is not the way of many marriages. Do not think that you have to find a gentleman that you care for in order to wed!"

Marie's fingers tightened all the more in her lap, now feeling a little painful. What was this about?

"But I am straying from the reason I am here to speak with you." Lady Stockbridge closed her eyes and let out a small sigh. "Marie, when you and I attended the wedding, I spoke at length with the Duchess of Wessex. We have become somewhat close acquaintances, since we spent so much of the Season together."

A tiny smile brushed Marie's lip. "She is a very lovely lady, I would agree."

"Indeed, she is. Though it is strange to me that her son should be so severe."

Marie nodded, wondering why her mother bit her lip and then looked away, as though she had said something she wished she had not. A little confused, she waited, only for her mother to nod briskly to herself, before addressing Marie again.

"The Duchess of Wessex made it quite clear to me that she thought *you* would be a suitable match for her son," she said, crisply. "Your father has subsequently written to the Duke of Wessex himself to see if he feels the same way and, having been invited to discuss the matter, has gone to his estate to do so."

It felt as though the solid seat she had been sitting on now evaporated to nothing, leaving her sinking into nothingness. Confusion battled at her heart, fear tearing it slowly, her stomach roiling, eyes flaring, sweat breaking out across her forehead.

Married?

"You need not look so shocked," her mother said, somewhat stiffly as though Marie's reaction to hearing this news was too severe and not worthy of her attention. "You know very well that we have been seeking a suitable match for you. You also know that it is difficult to do so when you are so clearly and plainly a bluestocking, for it is difficult for any gentleman of the *ton* to think well of an educated wife!"

This struck yet more fear into Marie's heart for what would the Duke of Wessex think of her love for reading and learning? She had only had one interaction with him thus far but it had not been a pleasant one. In fact, it had left her feeling cold and unhappy at his impropriety and ill manner.

And this was the gentleman she might marry?

"No." Closing her eyes, Marie shook her head as a chill stole over her, seeming to block out the warmth of the early afternoon sun. "I shall not."

Her mother clicked her tongue in disapproval. "My dear Marie, you must not be churlish."

"Churlish?" With her eyes damp, Marie looked back at her mother, her heart beginning to pound furiously, her hands clammy and mouth going dry. "Do you not know about the Duke of Wessex? Do you not know how ill a character he has? How he is dismissive of both his mother and of Martha? How he loves nothing more than solitude and cares nothing for the needs of others?"

Her mother's eyebrows lifted. "I know that all very well."

"Then why, if you even loved me a little, would you insist that I marry such a gentleman?" Marie asked, a single tear splashing to her cheek. "I understand that both you and father wish me to marry but must you force my hand in this way? Must you demand that I do such a thing?"

Lady Stockbridge turned her head away, as though she could not bear the sight of Marie's tears. "Marie, I hardly think that this is something you need speak so harshly about. If it is what the Duke desires, then all shall go well. It will be an excellent match, both for you *and* for him."

"How can you say such a thing?" Aware that her voice was rising but heedless to it, Marie dashed one hand over her eyes. "How could I possibly have any sort of happiness to a gentleman who is so cruel to his own sister and mother? How could I have any joy when he seeks nothing more than isolation? He may not want company but I certainly do... albeit not a great deal of it."

This made her mother's lips thin. "You have said the very thing that has encouraged me in all of this," she said, speaking a little more loudly now also.

"You do not care for company, for you prefer to read all that you can and learn as much as you can. That much is clear to me. The Duke of Wessex also does not care for company but he *does* require a wife. However, that wife must understand that he does not want often to be in conversation with her nor spend all of his time with her. Is that not what you would be contented with? He has a vast library that you could delve into at any time you chose and, given that there are a few noble families around his estate, you would be able to make strong connections with the other gentry also. That way, you can have your learning, your friends and your happiness, all whilst being wed to the Duke of Wessex." Her chin lifted, a spark in her eyes. "Just think, Marie! You would be a Duchess! Is that not significant?"

Marie closed her eyes. *Is that all that she wants for me? To have the standing and status of a Duchess?*

"This is a *good* match," her mother emphasized, as if Marie had not heard her say it the first time. "It may not go ahead regardless, my dear, for if the Duke of Wessex does not agree then all will be at an end anyway. And what need will there be for your upset at the present moment?"

Marie was caught between the urge to scream aloud at her mother for her lack of understanding or break down into sobs of sorrow and upset. She did neither, in the end, dropping her head low and gazing down at her hands as her shoulders rounded, a sense of hopelessness filling her.

"I am glad I was able to tell you. It will not come as such a surprise when your father returns home to tell you of what he was speaking of with the Duke." The rustling of skirts told Marie that her mother was taking her leave though she did not so much as lift her head, too overcome to raise her gaze to her mother's face.

"I shall leave you now and give you some time to consider your response to this," Lady Stockbridge said. "But do try to find a little bit of gratitude within your heart, Marie. It is for the best, I assure you."

The moment her mother stepped away from the arbor, Marie broke down completely. It was not that she could do anything or say anything that would prevent this from happening! It had already been decided and all without her consent, without her even being aware of it! Why had her father not come to speak with her *before* he had gone to the Duke? Why had he chosen not to speak a word to her? Would it not have been wise for her to have known something?

They did not want me to know, she realized, her eyes closing against the tears that were now streaming down her cheeks. *They knew what I would say. They knew I would object most strenuously and might have, somehow, changed my father's mind.*

Her father had always been kind to her, that much Marie could appreciate. Her mother had very often complained about her father's consideration of her, how he was encouraging to her reading and the like and thus, she had always expected that he would understand the sort of gentleman she would consider when it came to her marrying. That had certainly been the impression he had given her! Perhaps her mother, in seeing Lady Martha married, had encouraged him to do the opposite of his intentions.

It is pointless trying to find someone to blame, Marie thought to herself, uselessly attempting to wipe the tears from her eyes for more kept coming. *What is done is done and all I can do now is hope that the Duke will refuse to marry me.*

It was a faint hope but one that she clung to nonetheless. If the Duke refused to marry her, then the situation would come to an end and she would have no need for any upset, just as her mother had said.

But if he agreed, if he said that he would like to wed Marie, then she did not know what she would do.

Her life, as she knew it, would come to a short, sharp end, leaving her with nothing but darkness in her future.

Chapter Five

"It is told to me that your daughter is a bluestocking."

Rupert was a little surprised to see the flash in Lord Stockbridge's eyes at this remark, though he himself did not react to it. Surely the gentleman was ashamed of having a daughter so inclined towards bookish things! It was not the custom for young ladies. And any young lady in society who was considered a bluestocking, was generally looked upon with disfavour.

"My daughter has an excellent character and ought not to be poorly considered," Lord Stockbridge answered, firmly. "I myself do not find there to be any difficulty in this matter."

"Of her being a bluestocking?" Astonished, Rupert blinked in surprise as Lord Stockbridge nodded. "You care nothing for her reputation, then?"

Lord Stockbridge's hands clasped together in his lap though Rupert noted the way he gripped them so tightly, his knuckles whitened. He dismissed this, however, for if Lord Stockbridge wished to take offense in some manner, then Rupert did not care.

"I care for her *happiness*," Lord Stockbridge answered, his voice measured. "She finds great happiness in her reading and the like, and I certainly will not take that from her for the sake of society's expectations."

This gave Rupert pause. Clearly, Lord Stockbridge was not about to be criticized over his lack of consideration when it came to societal norms and, the more he considered this, the more Rupert himself began to think it was somewhat refreshing to hear. Though, that being said, he was not quite certain that having such a learned creature as his bride was something that he wanted.

"Nor would I expect that you, as her husband, would enforce her to stop what I have always encouraged," Lord Stockbridge continued, when Rupert said nothing. "To make things quite clear, Your Grace, I will *only* permit this match if there are particular stipulations and those written into a contract. I say that for the sake of my daughter's happiness which, in being wed to you, would be significantly lowered, I fear."

Rupert blinked in shock at the gentleman's remarks, utterly astonished that he would have spoken so to him. Did Lord Stockbridge not realize that he was addressing a Duke?

"You look surprised, Your Grace." Lord Stockbridge's lips lifted but there was no warmth in his expression. "You did not expect me to speak so, I presume."

"I most certainly did not!" Rupert exclaimed, about ready to have the gentleman dismissed from the house. "Do you truly think that you can demand such things?"

Lord Stockbridge levelled his gaze directly at Rupert. "Yes, I do."

This made Rupert's mouth go dry. If this was Lord Stockbridge's ill manner, then could he expect something similar from his daughter? That was certainly *not* what he desired in a wife.

"You have your own requirements, I understand?" Lord Stockbridge continued, putting a dent in Rupert's sudden ire. "Your mother and I spoke last evening, after my late arrival." One eyebrow lifted and Rupert flushed hot. He had chosen *not* to greet Lord Stockbridge upon his arrival, remaining in his own rooms rather than make his way to greet the fellow. It had not been particularly late either but Rupert had not had any desire to welcome Lord Stockbridge into his home and had, as he usually did, chosen isolation rather than company. It had been left up to his mother to greet Lord Stockbridge though Rupert had never once imagined that his mother would speak of such a thing as his conditions for the potential marriage between the two families.

"So," Lord Stockbridge continued, his voice a little lower now, "if you have your own particular... expectations then you will not have any difficulty in there being some for us also." His eyebrow lifted all the higher and Rupert, still feeling the heat in his face, had no other choice but to nod. What could he say? He could not refuse, could not state that no, the gentleman was not to have anything he desired for his daughter while he himself demanded one thing and the next!

"Excellent." Lord Stockbridge, looking quite satisfied, reached for the measure of brandy Rupert had offered him at the beginning of their conversation. "Then shall we discuss what these *provisions* might be?"

Rupert took in a slow breath and tried to quieten his thoughts which were pouring through him. "Indeed, we should. I shall begin." He did not give opportunity for the gentleman to disagree, nor did he offer him the chance to speak first. Certainly, it was rude but Rupert did not care.

"I will have my own chambers and my wife will have hers," Rupert continued, looking back at Lord Stockbridge now. "When I speak of chambers, I do not mean only bedchambers and the like, but rooms in the house I intend for her to keep to. There will be very few that will be shared."

"I see." Lord Stockbridge shrugged, much to Rupert's surprise. He had expected the gentleman to argue. "One of the rooms that is to be open to her must be the library, of course."

Rupert's brows knotted together. He did not much like being told what was going to happen and what he had to do. Was this all truly worth it? Was the match going to be all that he required it to be or would it bring him more stress and strain than ever before?

"You cannot hold that back from her," Lord Stockbridge said, firmly. "I shall demand the library be open to her."

"Very well." Tightening his grip into a fist in an attempt to keep his voice measured, Rupert looked away again. "She will not expect my company at any time of day or night. I shall give her my attention as and when I please and I am to be left in solitude whenever I desire for as long as I wish."

"And she will expect the same of you, then."

This sent a flame of irritation burning up Rupert's spine. "I beg your pardon?"

"Well, if she is to answer your summons, I daresay you should extend the same courtesies unto her." Lord Stockbridge smiled but his eyes did not warm. "Anything else?"

Feeling as though he were losing a grip on the conversation, Rupert cleared his throat and shook his head. If there were other things for him to discuss with the gentleman, they had completely gone from his mind. Though, at the very least, he had discussed the need for absolute privacy.

"Good. Then I shall tell you of my requirements." Lord Stockbridge lifted his chin, his blue eyes calm and steady. "You shall treat my daughter with respect at all times, giving her all that she desires in order to live a happy and contented life as a bluestocking. You will permit her opportunity to make friends with the gentry here in the surrounding area so she will not feel alone. You will permit her to come to call upon us and to reside with us for a prolonged holiday for as long as she desires. And you will, on no account, ever put a hand on her."

Shock flooded Rupert's heart like ice. "I can assure you, I would never set one hand – not even one finger – upon any other!"

Lord Stockbridge did not so much as blink. "I hope that is so, Your Grace. The truth is, I am not in the least bit acquainted with you and, given what I have heard, you can imagine my uncertainty over your character."

The shock began to melt away, turning to a bubbling anger instead. "What you have heard?"

"Of your isolation, your demanding nature and your selfishness," Lord Stockbridge answered, in that same blunt manner as he had shown before. "The only reason I am even considering this for my daughter is because, here, she will be able to be just as she desires – a bluestocking." His brow furrowed. "I could not imagine her in a marriage where her talents are ignored and squashed, where she is instructed to forget all that she has learned or where her desire to read and study is ripped from her. There are very few gentlemen in society who would be willing to even consider my daughter as their wife, fewer still who would encourage her bluestocking ways! But you, I think, might be all that she requires."

The edge of Rupert's lip curled. "Why not permit her to become a spinster?" he asked, a little harshly. "If no gentleman but myself will consider her, then why not let her do as she pleases... and accept the consequences that come with that."

Lord Stockbridge shook his head, a sadness coming into his eyes that bit back at Rupert's sharp tone. "You have no children as yet, Your Grace, so you cannot understand the depth of love that one has for one's own flesh and blood. I want what is best for Marie and what is best for her future is to be protected by a husband with standing and wealth. I cannot permit her to become a spinster for what happens to her when my wife and I are both gone from this world?" He shook his head. "I fear what would happen to her then though, if I were to say such a thing to her, I am sure she would reassure me with a firm gaze and determined words that she would do very well all on her own."

Rupert considered this but chose not to respond, seeing that there was more to this gentleman's intentions for his daughter than a mere desire to have all his children wed. He had not heard any gentleman speak of his children in such a manner and indeed, his own father had always been very dismissive and disinterested in both Rupert and his sister. That was why this explanation, this supposed *love* between father and daughter was such an unknown. He did not understand it, could *not* understand it and thus, could only return to the practicalities of the marriage, should it come to pass.

"I shall expect your daughter to treat me with respect and to do as I ask her," he said, his voice a little lower now as he fought to keep his emotions back. "I will not have her question me on any decision that I make nor any request I make of her."

The corner of Lord Stockbridge's lips twitched. "That is a fair and reasonable expectation," he said, with a nod, though nothing more was added to this. Did that mean something? Ought Rupert to be suspicious of it all?

"And she will not complain," Rupert finished, feeling a slight tension spin across his frame. "She will not question my lack of presence, my isolation and the like. She must understand that the only thing I want is solitude."

"I think she will not only accept that but be glad of it," came the reply. "Then are we in accord, Your Grace?"

Rupert hesitated, the question hitting him right between the eyes. Would he agree, then? Was he to marry Lady Marie?

"Your Grace?"

"If – if she agrees," Rupert found himself saying, stammering a little such was his doubt and confusion. "I shall not have a reluctant bride, Lord Stockbridge."

The gentleman nodded and got to his feet, clearly eager to bring the conversation to an end now that he had Rupert's agreement. "You shall not have her reluctant, I assure you," he said, with a small smile. "If she does not agree then the wedding shall not take place. I will return home now and discuss this all with her."

Rupert blinked. "Discuss it?"

"Of course. She must understand the reasons for my encouragements to wed! I will not have her thinking that I am demanding such a thing of her." His lips quirked, perhaps seeing Rupert's astonishment that any gentleman would do such a thing when they could easily demand that their daughter do as they said, just as Rupert would have expected most gentlemen of the *ton* to do. "I care for my daughter, as I have said. It is important to me that she sees all this clearly and makes the decision for herself. I shall inform you as soon as I can as to what her response will be. Good afternoon."

Before Rupert could form a single response, the gentleman had already quit the room, leaving him with the ever familiar and somewhat comforting solitude. He could hardly believe what he had just heard! He would have expected Lord Stockbridge to return home, inform his daughter about the betrothal and tell her when the wedding was to take place, not to ask her about her thoughts and her opinions! He was much too indulgent, Rupert considered, grimacing. Lady Marie, if she *was* to marry him, would soon learn that he was nothing like her father and never would be!

***

"Mother, if I might have a little solitude, I would appreciate it." Rupert scowled as his mother came into the drawing room, her head held high, clearly ignoring everything he had just said.

"You may not," she answered, sitting down in a chair opposite him as he brooded over a glass of whiskey. "You have not told me what you said to Lord Stockbridge and, given that he has taken his leave more than an hour ago, I must know what has been said."

Rupert rolled his eyes. "You are insistent, then."

"Yes," she said plainly and without concern. "I am."

Glaring at her in the hope that this would make her take her leave, Rupert waited in silence for what felt like an age before sighing loudly and looking away from her. Evidently, his mother was not to be moved.

"You may as well tell me, else I shall sit here with you for the rest of the day and again tomorrow," she said, quietly. "All I want to know is whether you are to wed or not."

Rupert rubbed one hand over his chin. It had been an hour since Lord Stockbridge had left him and still, he was not certain as to whether or not he had done the right thing. Even though they had been discussing the marriage, even though it had been nothing *but* the prospect of matrimony, Rupert had still found it a little surprising when Lord Stockbridge had asked him directly whether there would be a marriage or not. It had not been out of confidence and assurance that he had said yes but it had, strangely enough, come from a place of uncertainty and a dull sense of duty that bit down at him.

"Rupert?"

Closing his eyes, Rupert let her voice wash over him, aware that she had referred to him by his Christian name again. "Yes, Mother."

"Yes?"

Opening his eyes, he looked straight back at her. "Yes, I am to wed," he said, heavily, feeling not even the smallest sense of happiness or joy with it. "Though I have still to consider all that I require when it comes to it, for there will have to be a written agreement from both parties about what is both required and expected."

His mother nodded but there was no bright smile on her face, no delight in her eyes nor did she give him a joyous clap of her hands. Rupert frowned, pushing himself forward in his chair.

"I thought you would be pleased," he said, a little darkly. "After all, it was you who set this entire plan in motion, was it not?"

"And now I wonder if I have done wrong," she admitted, making his eyebrows lift in surprise. "Have I treated Lady Marie with inconsideration?"

"Inconsideration?" Rupert repeated, astonished. "Mother, she is to be a Duchess! How could you think such a thing?"

Her smile reappeared, yet it was not accompanied by warmth, but rather a touch of melancholy. "It is not the title that she will think of and neither is it what I consider," she answered, softly. "Indeed, I spoke of it all and indeed, I was the one who suggested it to Lady Stockbridge but now, seeing you as you are, I wonder if I erred. I thought, in truth, that you might be more amiable once you realised you were to have a wife! I thought you might be pleased and that, in itself, would bring you some freedom from this dark isolation you pull around you." She shook her head, her eyes closing as a sigh left her lips. "Yes, I spoke to you of the solitude that you so desperately seem to desire, suggesting that your wife would be able to give you that whilst, at the same time, providing an heir but, if I am to be honest, I did not ever think that you would desire it so greatly, you would have it written in a contract!"

"It must be in a contract; else how will she know what it is I expect of her?"

His mother opened her eyes. "She is to be your wife," she said, slowly, emphasizing each word. "I did not truly believe for a moment that you would so earnestly desire your isolation that you would have it written down and signed! I thought that your feelings might change, that you might have excitement and anticipation at the thought of being wed. I thought this might break through your dark spirits and –"

"So in brief, you attempted to manipulate me?" Rupert interrupted, growing angry now. "How could you do such a thing?"

"Because I want you to return to how you were," she answered, getting to her feet and making to come towards him, though she stopped short as he looked away from her. "You have held yourself in this guilt for too long, guilt that is not yours to bear! I have tried everything else I could think of to break you free from these chains but nothing has worked. I was sure that this, above all else, might be the thing to free you but now I fear I have been short sighted and foolish." Pulling out her handkerchief, she pressed it to her eyes. "And now I fear I have done Lady Marie harm."

"It is done now regardless," Rupert answered, firmly, his feelings all in disarray, coiling through him. "I am to be wed to Lady Marie and soon. Whatever your intentions were, whatever your hopes were to be, there is nothing now but what *I* want for my future alongside my wife." Seeing her about to say something more, he gestured to the door. "You may take your leave now, Mother. I do not want to have any further company for the remainder of the day."

His mother's tears came thick and fast this time but Rupert was unmoved. Much to his relief, she did as he had directed, turning around and making for the door. When the door closed behind her, Rupert let out a long breath and sank back into his chair, waiting for relief to fill him.

It did not come.

Instead, the only thing in his heart was pain.

Chapter Six

One month later.

"Come now, my dear. It is not usual for brides to be so broken by tears!"

Marie could only shake her head, blinking quickly to try and hide the tears her mother had already seen.

"You know that your father and I would not force you into this marriage," Lady Stockbridge continued, gently. "Why are you so sorrowful? You were the one who agreed to it, were you not?"

The knot in her throat prevented Marie from speaking. Yes, she wanted to say, she *had* agreed to this but it did not mean that her heart was contented at the thought. It had taken a full sennight of discussion and deliberation, of thinking and considering for Marie to have made her decision – and, on the whole, her agreement to this marriage had come solely because her parents both desired it for her. They did not know that, of course, for she would not have put such a burden upon their shoulders. They had spoken about the Duke at length, had made it clear about the stipulations he required and, much to her joy, the requirements her father had insisted upon also. She knew her husband was not to be a gentleman who would care for her. He was a man who wanted nothing more than solitude and to be left almost entirely alone, and that, she had feared, would leave her with loneliness and sorrow. But there had then come the reassurance of new acquaintances and, in time, friends from the local gentry. The Duke's mother would remain at the house for a time to make sure that she was introduced to them all.

That still had not convinced Marie, however. The Duke was, from what Martha had told her, dark tempered and disillusioned and she was a little fearful about what her future might look like with such a gentleman as her husband.

But I agreed to this, she told herself, as her mother pressed her handkerchief into her hand. *I said that I would wed him. I cannot turn back now!*

Looking back at her decision, Marie felt nothing but regret. She had been upset at the suggestion at first but when her father had explained all – including the contract with stipulations for both the Duke and herself – she had begun to soften. Her father had been concerned for her, as had her mother, but it was her father's gentle pleading that had torn at Marie's heart. She had seen his worry over what would happen to her should she remain unwed. A spinster had never been a thought that had troubled Marie but seeing her father's upset had made her reconsider. Of course, she had older siblings who had married and had families of their own and she had always thought that, should she remain unwed, she would go to reside with one of them... but her father had put an end to that thought. They might not want her company, he had explained. They might not desire her presence and feel her a burden upon them and that was not what he wanted for her.

And I told him I would accept the Duke's offer, Marie reminded herself, drying her eyes as best she could. *His concern and Mama's pleading pushed me to this decision. But how much I regret it now!*

"We must go." Lord Stockbridge patted Marie's hand, looking into her face. "We cannot turn back now, my dear. Trust me, all shall be well. You will have all the books you desire and will make a good many new acquaintances, I am sure."

Marie handed her mother her handkerchief, her eyes burning and fear clutching at her throat. The veil was set back in place and her father took her hand and set it on his arm, ready to step out into the church. This was to be the first time she had set eyes upon the Duke since her presence at his house for Martha's wedding. Her father had suggested a meeting before this day but the Duke had apparently thought it was not necessary and thus, there had been no conversation between them. Even that told her of his disinterest in her.

"You will soon see that there is nothing to worry about," her father said, gently. "Come, let us go."

"Yes, Father." It was all she could manage to say and with legs that felt as though she were dragging them, she turned to the door of the church. It was opened, the music filling the space as she was led forward by her father. The music was meant to be gentle and joyous but to Marie's ears, it whispered of darkness and sorrow. Her chest was tight, her breathing quickening as she walked down the aisle, seeing the guests on either side watching her arrival. They were smiling but she felt as though her heart was being torn apart. With great reluctance, she lifted her gaze to the gentleman she was to wed but the Duke of Wessex did not turn to look at her as any other gentleman might have done. Instead, he stood, his hands clasped behind his back and his face turned away from her instead of looking towards her.

Her heart shattered completely with regret coursing through her veins and pressing against her chest.

"Dearly beloved," the clergyman began, as the music stopped. "We are gathered together here in the sight of God, and in the face of this congregation, to join together this man and this woman in holy Matrimony; which is an honourable estate, instituted of God in the time of man's innocence, signifying to us the mystical union that is betwixt Christ and his Church; which holy estate Christ adorned and beautified with his presence, and the first miracle that he wrought, in Cana of Galilee; and is commended of Saint Paul to be honourable among all men: and therefore is not by any to be enterprised, nor taken in hand, unadvisedly, lightly, or wantonly, to satisfy men's carnal lusts and appetites, like brute beasts that have no understanding; but reverently, discreetly, advisedly, soberly, and in the fear of God; duly considering the causes for which

Matrimony was ordained. First, it was ordained for the procreation of children, to be brought up in the fear and nurture of the Lord, and to the praise of his holy Name. Secondly, it was ordained for a remedy against sin, and to avoid fornication. Thirdly, It was ordained for the mutual society, help, and comfort, that the one ought to have of the other, both in prosperity and adversity. Into which holy estate these two persons present come now to be joined."

A slight shiver ran down Marie's throat and she closed her eyes tightly. She did not want to think about that particular part of her requirement and duty as a wife. The Duke had made it clear to her father that he required the heir and the spare, which was just as she had expected, but how could she ever permit herself to be so very vulnerable with a gentleman such as he?

I will not have to give myself to him until I am ready, she told herself, firmly. *There will be locks on the bedchamber doors and I will keep them – and myself secure.*

So deep in thought was she that she did not realize that the clergyman had stopped speaking. A little panicked, she glanced first to her father and then to the Duke, though both were looking to the clergyman.

Then, he spoke again and he looked directly at Marie as she spoke, as if he had known she had not been paying attention. "Your Grace, Lady Marie. I require and charge you both, as you will answer at the dreadful day of judgment when the secrets of all hearts shall be disclosed, that if either of you know any impediment, why you may not be lawfully joined together in matrimony, you do now confess it. For be you well assured, that as many as are coupled together otherwise than God's Word doth allow are not joined together by God; neither is their Matrimony lawful. At which day of marriage, if any man do allege and declare any impediment, why they may not be coupled together in matrimony, by God's Law, or the Laws of this Realm; and will be bound, and sufficient sureties with him, to the parties; or else put in a caution to prove his allegation: then the solemnization must be deferred, until such time as the truth be tried."

If only I had something to say.

Realizing now that the silence had been due to the clergyman's request to the congregation to declare themselves if there was any reason for this marriage not to continue, Marie closed her eyes and prayed for relief. Was there something she might say now? Something that she could protest that would bring their engagement to an end? Of course, she had agreed to it and indeed, she had believed it to be the right thing for her to do but now, standing beside a gentleman who had not so much as glanced at her as yet made her worry she had made a terrible mistake.

"Then we come to the vows."

Another shudder ran through Marie and, out of the corner of her eye, she saw her father looking at her carefully. Could he tell just how troubled she was by this? Did he fear that she would step back and away from it all?

"Rupert, Duke of Wessex, will you have this woman to thy wedded wife, to live together after God's ordinance in the holy estate of matrimony? Will you love her, comfort her, honour, and keep her in sickness and in health; and, forsaking all other, keep only to her, so long as you both shall live?"

There came a long pause which, for a few moments, gave Marie a fierce hope, sending her heart into a furious, thundering rhythm. Would the Duke refuse? Would he step away and leave them both separate?

"I will."

Her eyes closed. *I do not believe you,* Marie thought to herself, daring a glance up at the Duke though he had his gaze turned steadfastly away from her. He would not love her, would not comfort and honor her, of that, she was quite sure. This was a marriage in name only. The Duke wanted to live as solitary a life as he could and it was her responsibility to make sure he was provided that.

Though, she considered, as the clergyman turned his attention to her, *neither shall I love him! In that, we are equal.*

"Lady Marie, will you have this man as your wedding husband, to live together after God's ordinance in the holy estate of matrimony? Will you obey him, and serve him, love, honour, and keep him in sickness and in health; and, forsaking all other, keep only to him, so long as you both shall live?"

Closing her eyes and praying that she was, somehow, making the right decision to accept this gentleman as her husband, she let out a slow, shuddering breath, the words escaping through her lips. "I will."

"Then who gives this woman to be married to this man?" The clergyman spoke quickly, as if he knew that Marie was feeling both confused and uncertain.

"I do." Her father pressed Marie's hand on his arm and then, catching her fingers, stepped back. When her hand was set on the Duke's arm, Marie's stomach roiled, threatening to cast up her accounts such was the state of her anxiety. But there was nothing she could do now. She had been given from her father to the Duke and now, the final vows were soon to be said.

"Your Grace, if you would repeat these words after me." With only a momentary pause, the clergyman continued. "I, Rupert, the Duke of Wessex, take you, Lady Marie, as my wedded wife; to have and to hold from this day forward, for better for worse, for richer for poorer, in sickness and in health, to love and to cherish, till death us do part, according to God's holy ordinance; and thereto I plight thee my troth."

The words were repeated but they were flat and dull, leaving Marie in no doubt as to how he truly felt about this marriage. Remorse was her constant friend now, standing beside her and nudging her heart with the knowledge that she had made a mistake in agreeing to this. Her eyes grew hot with tears and she blinked furiously, knowing she could not shame either herself or her family by breaking down into sobs.

When it was her turn to speak, the vows were said in nothing but a whisper, each one pulled from lips unwillingly. "I, Marie, take Rupert, Duke of Wessex, as my wedded husband, to have and to hold from this day forward, for better for worse, for richer for poorer, in sickness and in health, to love, cherish, and to obey, till death us do part, according to God's holy ordinance; and thereto I give thee my troth."

"And now, the ring."

A gentleman that Marie did not know stepped forward and handed the Duke the ring, though he barely acknowledged him. The feeling of the Duke's hand on hers did not bring Marie any sort of relief. Instead, as the ring was placed on her finger and the Duke murmured his words of promise, all she felt was a seeping coldness, going from her toes to the very top of her head. The Duke did not hold onto her hand as she had seen other gentlemen do on the day of their wedding. Instead, he let it drop back to her side, turning to face the clergyman rather than looking down at her. Thus far, he had not so much as even looked into her eyes!

This is what I am to expect, Marie reminded herself, as the clergyman began his prayer of blessing, something that she was sure they would need desperately. *My husband is to be a husband in name only. I already know that this is to be the way of things, do I not?* Steeling herself, Marie bowed her head and closed her eyes, barely hearing a word of the clergyman's prayer. *Even if I fear I have made a mistake in marrying this Duke, there is nothing that regret will do for me now. I must accept what I have and do all I can to improve upon it.*

"Oh eternal God, Creator and Preserver of all mankind, Giver of all spiritual grace, the Author of everlasting life; Send thy blessing upon these thy servants, whom we bless in thy Name; that, as Isaac and Rebecca lived faithfully together, so these persons may surely perform and keep the vow and covenant betwixt them made, whereof this Ring given and received is a token and pledge, and may ever remain in perfect love and peace together, and live according to thy laws; through Jesus Christ our Lord. Amen."

Marie looked up again, aware of the heaviness in her heart, a sadness that seemed to pervade every part of her. This was to be the final pronouncement. From this moment on, her life was to change in every way. She could only hope there would be even a sliver of happiness within it for her.

"Those whom God hath joined together let no man put asunder. For as much as the Duke of Wessex have consented together in holy wedlock, and have witnessed the same before God and this company, and thereto have given and pledged their troth either to other, and have declared the same by giving and receiving of a Ring, and by joining of hands; I pronounce that they be Man and Wife together, In the Name of the Father, and of the Son, and of the Holy Ghost. May God the Father, God the Son and God the Holy Ghost, bless, preserve, and keep you; the Lord mercifully with his favor look upon you; and so fill you with all spiritual benediction and grace, that you may so live together in this life, that in the world to come you may have life everlasting. Amen."

"Amen," Marie said softly, turning to look up at her husband but he was doing nothing but gazing directly at the clergyman, as though he was of significantly more importance than she was. In response, she dropped her head, only to become aware that the Duke had not lifted her veil. The clergyman had come to silence now, making Marie's face heat with embarrassment. Again, she turned to face the Duke, praying that he would notice his mistake and act quickly.

He did nothing but look to the clergyman.

Silence followed and Marie's whole body began to burn with shame. Everyone in the church was waiting for the Duke to do as he ought, to lift her veil and, by doing so, declare her to be his wife and still, he said nothing.

"Your Grace?" In a low voice, the clergyman leaned towards the Duke, his gaze flicking towards Marie before returning to him. "The veil?"

The Duke frowned. "What do you mean?"

"You must lift my veil," Marie answered, her voice a whisper. "Everyone is waiting."

With a curl of his lip and a flash of irritation in his eyes, the Duke turned to face her and, seemingly carelessly, grasped her veil with one hand and then flung it back over her head. It was done with no consideration, no carefulness and thus, it did not sit as it ought. Half of it was flung back, the other half twisted and draped itself over her face again though the Duke did nothing to assist. With a curl of his lip, he looked away from her, making Marie's heart tear with both the mortification of it all and the pain of his dismissal.

"Allow me."

The gentleman who had been standing next to the Duke, the ring-bearer, took it upon himself to come and make certain the veil was correctly placed. Marie could barely look at him, quite sure he would see the tears in her eyes and recognize just why she was so affected. With a whispered, 'thank you', she kept her gaze low as the gentleman returned to his place, leaving her with the Duke once more.

"The marriage lines must be signed," the clergyman said, though there was a slight frown on his face now rather than a look of happiness at having married them. "This way, Your Grace. And you also, Your Grace."

It was the first time that Marie had been referred to as such, the meaning not lost upon her. She looked up quickly, a breath catching in her chest as the clergyman held out one hand towards the side of the church. Hesitating, she waited for the Duke to step forward, wondering if he would offer to take her arm but, as she had expected, he did not. Instead, he made his way there directly, not waiting for her and certainly not looking over his shoulder to see whether or not she was following him. Marie did not think that she could feel any further shame, only for yet more to pour down upon her as she trailed after him. She could practically feel every eye upon her, sweat breaking out across her forehead as she followed after the Duke. Relief swallowed her as she stepped into the small room, the marriage lines waiting. It was even more of a relief to see her father coming to join them, glad that she was not to be alone with the Duke.

That was still to come.

As the marriage lines were signed and completed, the Duke of Wessex said not a word to her. The clergyman spoke more than either the Duke or herself and her father was watching on in silence.

"And now, the ceremony is at an end!" The clergyman beamed at the Duke, showing more emotion than she had seen in the service itself. "I am truly delighted to have been able to marry you today, Your Grace. It is a fine honour."

"Yes, I am aware of that and how it benefits you," the Duke said, with a sniff. "I do hope your congregation increases this Sunday... and the coffers with it."

The look of shock on the clergyman's face wiped away his smile in a single moment and Marie closed her eyes to hide the sight of his stunned expression from herself. Swaying slightly, her heart began to clamor within her, almost terrified as to what fate awaited her now. She had known of the Duke's character but to witness it, first hand, made her feel as though she was slowly sinking into darkness – darkness that would soon overwhelm her.

"The guests will be waiting."

Marie opened her eyes to see her father frowning back at the Duke, gesturing to her as he spoke.

"You must lead your wife outside."

"I know what I must do," the Duke responded, sharply. "Loathe though I am to do it."

With a nod, her father stepped away and the clergyman followed, leaving Marie and the Duke alone. It was an unwilling arm that was offered her and Marie, feeling the very same reluctance, set her hand upon it. The Duke started visibly the moment she touched him and Marie turned her gaze to the floor again, both horrified and upset at his reaction to her nearness. Was it a sense of aversion that made him flinch so? Distaste at being so close to her? She wanted to respond in kind, wanted to make it clear to him that she had just as little inclination towards him as he had for her... but nothing came to her lips.

"Very well." The Duke sighed audibly, seeming to speak aloud to himself. "It is done now. There is nothing for it but to present ourselves to the waiting guests." He snorted. "Though do not expect me to smile, Marie. I have no intention of pretending."

She looked up at him then, struck anew by the coldness in both his manner and in his expression. "In that, we are matched," she answered, her voice firm and not a dulled whisper, as she had feared. "Do not think for a moment that I desire this... or you."

The Duke narrowed his gaze, looking down at her with a sneer pulling at his lips. "Then it is just as well we shall be as separate as can be," he stated, sounding a trifle angry. "And the sooner that can begin, then all the better."

Chapter Seven

One week later.

Rupert frowned, running his finger down the column on the right-hand side of the paper. He was deep in thought, attempting to see which of the last three years had produced the best crops and, in doing so, wondering why it had been so. The weather had a good deal to do with it, indeed, but he had also begun to put more time and effort into considering such things. Given that he did not have any soirees or balls to attend, it gave him a good deal more time and that time had been used for productive engagements, such as reading about and implementing new ideas to see what might improve the soil.

A knock at the door interrupted him and Rupert, barely lifting his eyes from the paper, called for whoever it was to come in.

"Your Grace." The butler inclined his head. "Your wife wishes to speak with you."

Rupert waved a hand. "I am busy."

"Yes, Your Grace."

The butler departed without so much as a sound, leaving Rupert to continue on with his study though, much to Rupert's frustration, the fact that he had been interrupted seemed to pull much of his concentration away. Vexed, he set the quill down and leaned back in his chair, letting out a long, heavy sigh that did nothing but add to his frustration.

Why must she be so very exasperating?

He had only been wed near enough a sennight and already, her presence in the house was a constant niggle of irritation. It was not as though she interrupted him often nor that they spoke at length every day – in fact, they had only had one brief conversation and that had been in the carriage on their way back to his estate when Rupert had been too weary to continue riding alongside her. They had shared only a few minutes of conversation, a conversation where he had made it quite clear that their stipulations were of the utmost importance to him and one where he had made it very clear indeed that he wanted nothing more than to be left alone and that had been all. Frowning, Rupert closed his eyes and rubbed one hand over them, the way she had looked back at him as he had spoken burned into his memory. Her green eyes had been a little glassy, her face pale with no hint of color in her cheeks. The way her dark hair had been pulled back from her face made her appear all the more unwell and Rupert had been a trifle concerned that she might cast up her accounts in the very carriage itself and ruin it, though that had not come to pass. Upon their arrival at the house, he had left her in the care of the housekeeper and had made his way to his own chambers, relieved to be free of the lady he was now to call his wife.

A lady I do not want in this house, he reminded himself, his lips flattening. *But a lady that is present nonetheless.*

Sighing aloud again, Rupert took in a few long breaths in an attempt to calm and quieten his frustrations, though it did not do a great deal. Why had she interrupted him? What could possibly be of such great importance that she had sent the butler to him?

Looking down at his papers, Rupert let out a groan of frustration and, getting to his feet, stalked to the door. Wrenching it open, he stomped out into the hallway and turned his feet in the direction of the drawing room, sure that was where she would be.

She was not.

Growing all the more irritated, Rupert caught the attention of a nearby footman. "The Duchess. Where is she?"

"She is in the library, Your Grace," the footman answered, his eyes fixed to the floor in a sign of deference. "Shall I fetch her for you?"

Rupert ignored this and hurried along the hallway towards the library. He ought to have guessed that was where the lady would be but given that he had spent little time in her company and certainly had not any interest in her, he had not thought of it. Pushing open the door, he stepped inside, his hands curling into fists in order to contain his growing anger.

"What do you think you are doing?"

The Duchess jumped in surprise at the sound of his voice, turning sharply from her position over a small pile of books. "Your – Your Grace," she stammered, her hands clasping in front of her. "I did not think you would come to speak with me. I thank you for –"

"Oh, I have not come because of your request," he interrupted, aware of just how loud his voice was but caring nothing for it. "I have come because the butler's interruption on *your* behalf has caused me to forget all that I was doing and has taken away my concentration entirely! There is no reason for you to do such a thing and I will insist that you never do such a thing again!"

As Rupert's voice faded, Marie stood taller than he had ever seen her before. With a lifted chin and a steady gaze in his direction, she folded her arms over her chest and narrowed her eyes.

Rupert's heart slammed hard in his chest, battling fury.

"I have every right to come and speak with you," she said, in a tone that brooked no argument though Rupert had every intention of doing so. "You are my husband and there are, on occasion, matters that will require me to speak with you."

"Then you will wait for a suitable time," he said, taking a step closer, knowing that he could tower over her if he so wished. "*I* shall tell you when I am ready to hear all of your ills, when I am able to listen to your complaints."

"You expect me just to wait?" Her eyebrows lifted. "And what if you do not wish to speak with me for six months?"

He shrugged. "Then you will wait for six months."

The lady blinked, then let out a cold, hard laugh, turning her head away from him. "Wait for a time when *you* feel able to speak? To share what it is that troubles me?"

"Yes." Another shrug lifted his shoulders. "It is not as though I wish to have any conversation with you, Marie. Or have you forgotten that?"

This brought a touch of red to her cheeks. "I have not forgotten anything, believe me," she said, her voice low, her eyes holding his rather than pulling away, as he might have expected. "But you are being entirely unreasonable to expect me, as your wife, to remain silent unless *you* have desire to speak to me. This is now my house as much as it is yours and —"

"And you are still under my authority," he spat, shaking one finger at her as his anger began to burn. "*I* shall tell you when I have both the time and the inclination to listen to you. You will not send for me again."

Her eyebrows lifted and she did not step back nor quail as he might have expected. Instead, his harsh words appeared to encourage her defensiveness, her eyes flashing as she remained before him.

"I shall do just as any wife is permitted to do and seek to speak with my husband whenever I have need."

"Then I shall always refuse, for it is my right to give you my time and my presence as and when I choose."

A tiny hint of a smile touched one corner of her mouth, making Rupert's anger fade just a little. Why, in heavens name, was she smiling? Why did she appear to be so jovial when he had just finished berating her?

Refusing to entertain any further thoughts of her and certainly having no intention of asking her why she was smiling, Rupert swung around and pushed back through the library door, thundering back through the hallway and desperate now to be back in his own study *without* interruption.

I shall have to tell the butler that no-one is to interrupt me again, not unless it is a matter of life or death.

"Ah, there you are."

Rupert stopped short, only to shake his head and make to move past his mother. "I have no time for conversation, Mother."

"Did you speak with your wife?"

"No. I do not want to." He did not look back at her, making still for the study door though he knew full well his mother would follow after him.

"I see. Well, I shall tell her to continue on regardless then, until you are able to speak with her."

This, despite Rupert's own anger, made him stop walking. Turning his head slowly, he looked back at his mother, his brows falling low over his eyes. "What do you mean?"

"The library." She smiled warmly at him. "Your wife is quite lovely, is she not? It was her idea to rearrange the library books so that they were all sorted into an easier and more suitable situation. I said that she was to continue on since you would not care but her desire was to make sure you were comfortable with the notion."

"Oh." Rupert's shoulders dropped, as did his frown. "There is no need for her to do such a thing, however. I am quite certain all is just as it ought to be."

At this, the Dowager Duchess snorted. "I hardly think so, Wessex. You have not set foot in that library for months!"

"That is not true at all." Rupert scowled back at her, aware that the truth behind her words was there all the same. Indeed, he *had* stepped into the library but it had not been to read. It had been a quiet place, at times, for him to escape to. Many a time, he had sat beside the open fire, whiskey in hand as he had gazed into the flickering flames and wondered just how long his guilt would torment him.

"Nonsense." His mother waved a hand, dismissing him. "You have not touched a book on those shelves in years. I shall tell her to continue on, though I shall not be present to see it at its conclusion." Her smile was a little sad. "I shall miss your wife a good deal when I remove to the Dower house."

Rupert's lips flattened. "Remind me when that is to be?"

Her eyes shifted to his again, the sadness in her expression lingering. "In five days time, though I am sure you wish it would be sooner," she said, softly. "But you will not rid yourselves of us for long. Your sister and I are to call upon you here very soon, for both of us wish to make sure that your wife is neither lonely *nor* sorrowful."

"I care not." Rupert shrugged his shoulders and then turned around again. "You may do as you please, it will not make me change my ways." In his heart, he knew all too well that he did not want his mother nor his sister to return to visit here but to say that aloud would do no good. In fact, Rupert was sure it would only make her all the more determined to do so. "Now, do excuse me."

"Though I shall also return to reside here for a longer time when the first baby is born," his mother called after him, making a chill run down Rupert's spine. "I do hope that an announcement will be forthcoming very soon. You need the heir, Wessex!"

Opening the study door, Rupert stepped inside, closed it again and then turned the key. Closing his eyes, he leaned back against the door and breathed out slowly, aware of the wriggle of discomfiture that ran down his spine.

Marie was his wife and he had every right to come to her bedchamber but he had not yet done so. He could not be certain what had impeded him, but, much to his vexation, he acknowledged that his mother was correct. The heir *was* required and he ought not to delay.

Grimacing, he rubbed one hand down his face and then, pushing away from the door, he returned to his study desk. *Tonight,* he told himself, glancing across the room to where his whiskey and brandy stood. *Once it is dark, I shall approach.*

The way his heart twisted and his stomach roiled told Rupert that he was not particularly keen to follow through with his intentions but it was required of him nonetheless. It was not that he lacked awareness of what was anticipated of him; rather, he was utterly unacquainted with the lady herself, and thus, it rendered him both discomposed and uncertain. The last thing he wanted was to cause her any sort of physical pain but she had to be expecting him to come to her bedchamber! Mayhap she was wondering why he had not! After all, it had been discussed with her, made clear to her that the heir and spare were required, so why would he refrain?

"I shall not refrain," he said, firmly, the sound of his voice echoing around the study. "I shall go to her tonight and my duty, I must hope, shall soon be done."

Chapter Eight

"Your Grace?"

It took Marie a moment to realize that the maid was speaking to her, given that she was so accustomed to being referred to as, 'my lady'. Turning in her seat, she beckoned the maid forward.

"Thank you, Your Grace." The maid bobbed a curtsy, then handed her a note. "Is there anything else I can fetch for you this evening?"

Marie took the note, a little confused as to who it would be writing it. "No, I thank you. I am ready to retire now, I think." She waited until the maid quit the room before returning her attention to the note. How very strange! Who would be sending her a note from within this house? Surely it would not be the Duke, which meant that it was the Dowager Duchess... though they had sat together earlier that evening, so why had she not said anything then?

Frowning, Marie unfolded the note and read the few short words.

Her breathing hitched, one hand flying to her mouth as her eyes rounded. Panic began to fill her, spreading outwards from her chest as her eyes, fixed and staring, centered on only two words.

'Be ready.'

Her eyes closed as Marie took in quick, sharp breaths. It had been over a sennight now since their wedding day and the Duke had never once come to her rooms.

Now, evidently, he was planning on doing just that.

'I will come to you this evening', the note had said. 'Be ready.'

She shook violently at the thought of her husband coming to her, expecting her to do just as he bade her. Indeed, it was a part of their marriage and indeed, it was expected of her but could she truly give him just as he required? No, Marie thought to herself, she did not think she could.

Recalling their interaction earlier in the day only made Marie shudder again, her eyes closing and one hand gripping the arm of the chair as though somehow, it would stabilize her. She and the Dowager Duchess had been enjoying an excellent conversation about books and the like, and she herself had expressed a desire to rearrange all of the books in the Duke's library, wanting to make sure they were all in the correct order. She had pointed the state of the library out but pulling out two books from the same shelf, one which was the history of King Edward the first, and the other, a novel of love and intrigue. The Dowager Duchess had laughed and encouraged her to do as she pleased but Marie had been hesitant. She had not wanted to add to the Duke's frustration and anger by doing something he had not agreed for her to do and thus, she had sent the butler to him.

The butler's return to her and his explanation that the Duke was very busy indeed and could not spare his time had made her both upset and irritated. The Dowager Duchess had taken her leave at that moment in order to take the air, though Marie had wondered if it was the lady's frustration with her son's response that had required such a thing.

And then, the Duke had returned.

Even now, Marie could still hear the way his voice had filled the room, bouncing off the walls and crying foul over her supposedly heinous crime of sending the butler to him. She had been determined to protect herself, however, and had done so without hesitation. The Duke had not been pleased with that, she knew, but neither did Marie care. Her own reputation was of no significance any longer and thus, she could say and do just as she pleased.

Could I not do the same now?

A momentary burst of hope flung itself across her chest, only for Marie to frown and close her eyes. She could not do that, could she?

But why not?

Her stomach twisted but Marie nodded to herself, rising to her feet and feeling the tremble in her limbs as she did so. On her wedding day, had she not told herself that she would close the door to him and refuse to permit him entry until she herself felt ready for his nearness?

"And," she said to herself, beginning to make her way to the connecting door between her bedchamber and the Duke's bedchamber, "did he not say to me that it was his right to give me his time and his presence whenever he chose? Why should that not be the same for me?"

It would not bring any sort of harmony nor delight between them, that much Marie knew full well. All the same, she did not intend to permit the Duke to take just as he pleased, without feeling or consideration! He did not appear to be a gentleman who would give her any thought whatsoever, given that he had displayed that callousness towards her on more than a few occasions.

Making sure the connecting door was closed tightly, Marie turned the key in the lock and then pulled it back, gripping onto it. The key was fairly large but she could not be sure that there was not another one in the Duke's possession. If there was, then how could she escape him? Could she protest and refuse? She shivered, her eyes closing for a moment as fear clutched at her. Would he demand it of her? Insist, to the point of forcing himself upon her?

I must find a way.

Looking around the room, Marie went to ring the bell to summon the maid. The first thing to do was to find out whether the Duke of Wessex had a key to the connecting door and to the door of her bedchamber itself. If he did not, then she would be able to secure herself in her bedchamber without any further effort. But if he did, then she would have to think of something else she might be able to do in order to ensure that she was kept back from him – and that he could not break his way in.

***

Fingers twisting in her lap, Marie's lips broke open with a cry of surprise as the handle of the connecting door turned sharply. The glass of brandy she had poured for herself was near enough empty but it still did not take away all of her fear.

"Marie." The Duke's voice was loud and commanding. "Open this door at once."

Rising to her feet, Marie walked to the door and, closing her eyes, spoke with as much firmness as she could muster. "I am afraid I cannot do so."

"You must." The authority in the Duke's voice told her that he was not about to accept her refusal without difficulty. "I have already told you to be prepared for my arrival."

Licking her lips, Marie kept her eyes closed tightly. "I am afraid I cannot." She shivered lightly as the Duke rattled the handle again.

"Where is the key?"

Marie, drawing in both strength and air, set her shoulders back and opened her eyes. There was nothing for her to be afraid of, she reminded herself. Not only did she have the key to the connecting door *and* to the door of her bedchamber, but she had also had the maid fetch her a wedge to push into the small gap between the door and the floor. Even if the Duke *did* somehow manage to unlock the door, he would not be able to enter. In fact, she had been promised, the harder he pushed, the more fixed it would become.

"As I have said, I am afraid I cannot permit your *arrival* into my chambers this evening," she said, aware of the slight tremor in her voice and hating the sound of it. "I understand that you expect me to do just as you demand but, in this case, I shall not."

There was a momentary pause. Marie's skin crawled with the tension rattling up and down her spine, fearful of the tirade that was soon to follow. What she anticipated quickly came to pass, for the Duke not only turned the handle in a furious manner, but he also began to pound on the door, making her jump, her hands flying to her mouth.

"You have no right to deny me! You are my *wife* and under my authority and that means you will do just as I command! Open this door at once! Open it now, else I shall fetch the housekeeper and take the key from her... and woe betide you when I do!"

Marie, shaking now, shook her head as though he could see her. "You will not threaten me, Your Grace," she answered, relieved that she had enough strength still to speak with force. "Nor will you put a hand upon me. If you do, then I shall return to my father and the shame that will follow will be significant." She did not use the word 'separation' but that was precisely what she intended. If the Duke ever put one single bruise upon her, then she would return home and have her father organize a legal separation. To do such a thing would be shameful for her, indeed, but it would also bring a good deal of shame to the Duke and his family name. Not many gentlemen would dare risk such a thing and, as she spoke those words, the Duke appeared to quieten a little.

Another thump came to the door. Then another, making it sound as though he was throwing his whole weight behind the door.

Then there came silence for some minutes, making her quake inwardly.

"You have no right to bar me," he said, his voice a little more measured now. "This is not what I demanded nor expected."

Drawing in a long breath, Marie clasped her hands together under her chin in an attempt to stop herself from shaking. "Nor is it what I expected," she said, aware of just how much she still trembled. "But if I desire to speak with you and you tell me that you will only converse with me at a time that *you* are satisfied with, then I shall hold the same standard for myself."

Silence met her words but Marie continued without hesitation, growing a little stronger with every word she said.

"I recall the words you said." Closing her eyes and silently hoping she remembered his response correctly, she spoke quickly so he would not have time to defend himself. "You said, 'I shall tell you when I have both the time and the inclination to listen to you. You will not send for me again." She snatched a breath. "Therefore, if that is what you hold me to, then I hold you to the same. I shall tell you when I have the time and the inclination for your company, in *any* form, Your Grace. Do not demand that I prepare myself for your presence again."

Nothing more was said. Marie watched with trepidation as the handle of the door was turned once more – although calmly this time – before it was released entirely. Then, after another few seconds of silence, she heard the Duke's footsteps fading as he walked away from the connecting door.

She sank to the floor in a heap, her frame trembling with terror and her skin prickled with the chill of dread. Tears burned in her eyes and she let them fall, her hands covering her face so she could hide the sobs from him, should he be able to hear her. Quite how long she stayed there for, Marie did not know. All she could hear was her heartbeat, silence telling her that she was safe, that she was secure... for the time being at least.

But what would she face come the morning? Marie trembled at the thought. Would the Duke's anger be thrown over her at the breakfast table? At luncheon? Or would he come in search of her at a time she did not expect, surprising her with his presence *and* his fury?

"I am safe now," she whispered to herself, her hands dropping from her face but only so she could wrap her arms around her knees. "For the moment, at least, I am safe."

Chapter Nine

Rupert threw both hands through his hair, aware that his hair was now wild and furious but he did not care. Striding through the gardens, he turned this way and that, heedless to where he was going but driven only by anger.

How dare she refuse me?

He had slept only a few, fitful hours last night, tossing and turning as he had tried to find any sense of peace that might help him drift into slumber. That had not come to him, making his frustration grow all the more. Now, in the early hours of the morning, he found himself walking through the gardens, doing his utmost to free himself of the fury which still bound itself to him.

She has no right, he told himself, his breath frosting the air. *She is my wife! I must be permitted to take my conjugal rights, regardless of her feelings.*

A small stab of conscience gave him pause, dampening some of his fury. Would he truly have gone to her bed when she was reluctant and unwilling? Would he have demanded, in no uncertain terms, that she do as was expected? Stopping short, Rupert dropped his head and let out a slow breath, running both hands through his hair again.

No, he would not have done so. That much he knew to be true. The whole idea was, in itself, already filled with tension and strain for he did not know the lady in any way whatsoever and yet was meant to step forward so he might know her in the most intimate way possible!

"All the same," he muttered, darkly, "she should never have locked the doors between us."

She did so to protect herself from you.

That thought came unbidden and made Rupert scowl, his brow furrowing and his chest tight. Did Marie truly believe that he would have forced her to his bed? Was that what she thought of him? Then again, Rupert considered, it was not as though she had any understanding of his character or the like, so it might well be that she thought such a thing of him.

And it was not as if I showed her any consideration. His lips twisted. His note had practically demanded that she be prepared and ready for him without ever once speaking with her face to face about the matter.

"Wessex!"

A voice broke through the quiet of the gardens and Rupert frowned, seeing his mother coming towards him. "What in heaven's name are you doing out at this hour?"

"This hour?" His mother came to stand directly in front of him, her hands on her hips and her eyes narrowed as she looked up at him. "It is already past the hour to break your fast and I have been told that you have been out walking since before the sun rose."

His irritation burned hot. "I can do just as I please, Mother. If you have forgotten, then I shall remind you that I am the Duke of Wessex and I am well able to do just as I desire without the need for any remarks or rebuffs from you."

This made her eyebrows lower, shadows sitting in her eyes. "Oh, it is not because of that, Wessex. It is not your early morning perambulations that occasion my presence. It is because of your wife."

Rupert's heart fell to the ground. "What of her?"

"Have you seen her?"

He shook his head. "No." He did not say a word about how he had spoken with her the previous evening, thinking to himself that such a conversation was nothing to do with his mother. "What is the trouble, Mother?"

"The difficulty lies in the fact that her lady's maid entered the bedchamber this morning to discover your wife fainted upon the floor near the adjoining door to your apartments."

Fear lurched in Rupert's frame.

"She was white as could be and could not seem to stand on her own. I was sent for at once, for fear that a physician would be required but it seems that the poor girl is only very chilled from sitting where she was and, with some warmth and sustenance, she is recovering well." Her eyes glinted with a sharpness that betrayed her upset. "What did you do, Wessex? I may have mentioned about the heir but I did not ever think that you would treat your wife in such a vicious way in order to bring that about!"

Shock flung itself at Rupert's chest and for a few moments, he could not speak. His mother's face was pale save for a slowly increasing flush of red in each cheek and Rupert, horrified, was quick to correct her.

"No, I did nothing of the sort! That is not to say that I did not attempt to make my way into her bedchamber but she had locked the door."

A long breath escaped his mother's lips, her eyes closing. "Goodness. That is something of a relief, I suppose."

"I am not the sort of gentleman who would ever do such a thing!" Rupert waited for his mother to say that indeed, she knew he was not and that she was sorry for having ever thought such a thing but neither of those things were said. Instead, she gave him a somewhat assessing look as if trying to decipher what was true and what was not and Rupert's heart tore.

Is that truly what she thinks of me?

"I thought you knew me better than that," he growled, pushing away his upset and turning it into anger instead. "How could you ever suggest such a thing about me?"

His mother lifted her shoulders and then let them fall. "I do not know you as well as I once did," she said, her voice quiet but her words as loud as thunderclaps. "You have altered so severely, I cannot be sure what you would or would not do."

Rupert's mouth went dry as he fought to find a way not only to defend himself but to reassure her, but there was nothing he could say. *Have I truly changed so much?*

"That does not explain why your wife was found in such a state, however," his mother continued, before he could respond. "The maid said that she had never seen her in such a way before and therefore, there must be a reason as to why she was so."

"If there is, then I cannot see why that is any of your concern," he answered, a trifle stiffly. "She is *my* concern and mine only."

At this, the Duchess not only snorted but rolled her eyes in an obvious manner. "As though you are showing her any care or consideration!" she exclaimed, throwing up her hands. "I hardly think that *you* are going to be kind and generous towards her, are you? You are not going to go to her with gentleness, eager to know what it is that has troubled her so, are you? Do not pretend for a moment that you have any interest in your wife, for I know that you do not and nor do you intend to show her any either." She shook her head again, though Rupert noticed the glistening tears in her eyes. "I should never have suggested this. How much I regret now informing you about Lady Marie. How much I regret even making this arrangement! If I had known that you would be so very cruel towards her, then I would not have done such a thing."

"Cruel? I am not cruel!" Rupert exclaimed, throwing up his hands. "I am not in the least bit cruel! I have done nothing to injure her, have not set one hand to her."

His mother shook her head. "I do not know if I can believe that. And even if you were not so, then I can promise you that your words would have been more than a little hurtful towards her."

Setting his jaw, Rupert shook his head and looked away. "I am sure she is quite well. You cannot know what my words have been to her nor can you tell me what effect they would have had upon her."

"Oh yes, I can." The softness in his mother's voice gave Rupert pause, his eyes turning back to look at her. When she finally returned her gaze to his, there was such a sadness in her expression, such a weight upon her that it seemed to shrink her in stature, right before his eyes. "I know exactly the damage that can be done by your words, my son. I know it first hand and I can tell you that your wife will be bearing just as much of an injury as I." Turning on her heel, she made to walk away, only to spin back around to face him. "Oh, and I shall not be taking my leave of this house as intended. Not until I can be sure that Marie is safe enough and happy enough for me to depart."

"What?" Rupert exclaimed but his mother did not appear to hear him. Either that or she had no intention of responding to his remarks, given the hurried steps she took to get away from him. He watched her as she made her way back towards the house, anger beginning to twist through him again. It was a very familiar emotion, one that he contended with near every day but Rupert still did not manage it well. It made him grow hot and flustered, his hands curling up, his chest tight, his jaw set. Narrowing his gaze at his mother's back, he ignored all the whispers of his conscience, fully aware of what it was that was being said to him. Over and over, he rejected it, pushing it away as his anger took an even greater hold of him.

This is her *fault,* he told himself, as his conscience tried to roar loudly over him. *My mother is the one who brought Marie here. Marie is the one who turned me away last evening. None of this is my doing.* Raising his chin, Rupert scowled darkly, rubbing one hand over his face. *I shall take no responsibility for it is not mine to take. I have enough guilt already.*

***

"Marie."

Despite the fact he had spent a good deal of the day telling himself he had nothing to apologise for, that he was quite right in all of his actions and that it was both his mother and Marie at fault, Rupert found himself standing at the door of the library, hoping that this conversation with his wife would bring him all the peace he needed. His thoughts were too many, coming into his mind repeatedly as he fought to keep his conscience at bay.

"Marie?" Again, he said her name but this time, he pushed the door open just a little. The lady was sitting in a chair by the fireplace, book in hand and a tea tray in front of her. Steam rose gently from the tea cup beside her and Rupert took a moment to pause, seeing the scene as somewhat idyllic and, strangely enough, a little reluctant to break the quiet. His gaze went to his wife, taking her in as she read. Clearly, she was utterly absorbed in whatever it was she was reading, meaning that his presence was not even noticed.

She is rather beautiful.

The thought was not one that he had expected and it struck at him, hard. Rupert snatched in a breath, taking the thought and flinging it far from him. He could not let himself think such ridiculous things! The last thing he desired was to have any sort of connection with his wife and to see her in that sort of favorable light would do neither of them any good.

The sound of him catching his breath caused the lady to glance upward, and nearly letting her book slip from her fingers, her eyes widened with terror.

"Marie." Seeing this, Rupert came a little further into the room but stood behind another chair, making no move to come closer to her. "Good afternoon."

"Good afternoon." A slightly choked sound followed these words, as if she were trying to say more but could not find the right thing to say. Rupert looked back at her, relieved that, at the very least, she was meeting his gaze.

"I wanted to speak to you about last evening," he said, doing his best to keep his tone even. "You cannot keep me from your bedchamber, Marie."

Her chin lifted a notch, though her face was pale. "Yes, I can. And I shall until I feel that we are a little better acquainted… and until you begin to treat me with some consideration."

"This is not a negotiation!" Rupert thumped the top of a chair with one fist, his anger beginning to spike again. "I am your husband and I have every right to take you to my bed."

The lady looked away, a hint of color in her cheeks now. "I am not denying you that right, Your Grace. The heir must be produced. I understand that but I simply shall *not* permit you to treat me as if I am a possession that you will take and then discard whenever you please." Her eyes closed for a moment before, with a deep breath, she looked back at him. "I shall treat you as you treat me, Your Grace. I cannot see why that causes you such difficulty."

Rupert gripped the top of the chair, his fingers whitening. "Because I have the right to your company, Marie."

"Just as I, as your wife, have the right to *your* company and conversation, though that is not given," she responded, sharply. "You will remind me of our agreement, no doubt, and I will state now that I have every intention of giving you as much solitude as I can. But I should be able to come and speak with you on the rare occasion that I require to do so, without being pushed away or told that you will speak to me only when *you* are ready and when *you* desire it."

There were plenty of things that Rupert wanted to say to this, a good many things that he desperately wanted to tell her in response but none of them would offer her a fair and reasoned reply. They would only be sharp, angry remarks or biting scoldings that would try to make her feel as shamed as possible. Indeed, that was what he usually said – or did – without hesitation but after his mother's words to him earlier in the day, Rupert felt himself held back.

Which was more than foolish.

"I shall have the key from the housekeeper," he stated, a glint in his eye. "I was not able to fetch it last evening given the lateness of the hour but I shall do so today."

Marie lifted one eyebrow, though Rupert noticed how she clasped her hands tightly in her lap. Was it fear that caused her to do so? He did not want her to be afraid of him… so why was he saying such threatening things?

"You may have the key, Your Grace," she answered, her voice so quiet that Rupert had to strain to hear her, "but even then, you will find the doors barred to you. If I must force you, by my own strength, to hold yourself to the same standard as you hold me to, then I shall do precisely that."

Rupert did not know what the lady meant by *her own strength* but the confidence in her gaze and her quiet reply unnerved him. Besides which, he recognized, he did not *want* her to feel any sort of dread when she was around him. Surely, he wanted to be respected and certainly, he wanted her to abide by all that they had agreed but to be afraid? No, he considered. He did not want that.

"Then you leave me no choice," he muttered, turning away from her. "I came here in the hope of having your agreement and your understanding. Instead, I see that you are nothing but stubborn, selfish and heedless to the requirements your standing as my wife brings you."

"On the contrary, Your Grace."

Rupert turned around sharply, astonished that she thought to respond to him.

"I am mindful of my requirements as your wife. Neither am I selfish, else I would never have agreed to marry you in the first place. Stubborn, however?" She tilted her head, the fear in her eyes no longer hiding there. "Indeed, I suppose that I am, for I have determined to hold you to the same ideals as you hold for me. However, that can change, the moment that you decide to treat me with a little more consideration." Her head straightened, her eyes sharp now. "I wonder, then, who is the one to be considered stubborn, Your Grace? You or I?"

The audacity of the lady made Rupert's mouth drop open. She held his gaze for another moment, then lifted her book and, opening the page, began to read – and all while he stood there! How did that show him any sort of respect? How dare she do such a thing? His heart burned hot within him and he was about to stride forward and throw blistering, burning words towards her for her boldness, only for a vision of his mother's sorrowful face to come to his mind. What was it she had said to him?

I know exactly the damage that can be done by your words, my son. I know it first hand and I can tell you that your wife will be bearing just as much of an injury as I.

His eyes closed tightly, his breathing ragged as he swung between two reactions. The first was to do just as he wanted, to rail at her in the most furious manner, whilst the other told him to turn on his heel and walk from the room without saying another word.

Still breathing hard, Rupert let out an exclamation of frustration but did as he did not *want* to do. Turning around, he threw open the door of the library, hearing it crack against the wall behind him. He did not care, did not stop to make sure it was closed properly but instead, stormed down the hallway, his fury still writhing within him.

She is utterly infuriating, he thought, his face hot. *How am I ever to put up with her?*

Chapter Ten

"Marie? Might I ask you something?"

Marie nodded, reaching for her tea as the Dowager smiled back at her. "Of course."

"Are you... are you quite well?"

A little surprised at the Dowager's question, Marie nodded, looking back at her in confusion. "Yes, of course I am. Why do you ask?"

Hesitating, the Duchess looked away for a few moments. "It is only because the maids came to me somewhat concerned."

Marie frowned. "When?"

"Yesterday. In the morning."

Realizing in an instant what it was that the Duchess referred to, Marie waved a hand, a little embarrassed. "I am quite well. It was foolish of me to fall asleep where I sat."

"And that is the only reason, is it not?" The Duchess' eyes were keen. "You slept in an awkward position?" When Marie nodded, the Duchess frowned. "Might I ask why you were there?"

Now it was Marie's turn to hesitate. What ought she to say? She could not simply inform the Dowager that the Duke wanted to bed her and that she had chosen to refuse! That might make her think very poorly of her indeed.

"I should not have asked." Seeing her pause, the Dowager smiled briskly. "It does not matter. It does not concern me, I suppose."

"I am grateful for your consideration and your understanding," Marie answered, reaching for her tea again and watching the Dowager's face. "If you are in any way concerned that the Duke injured me in some way, I can assure you that I have never been physically injured by him. That is not the cause of my... foolishness for falling asleep in that strange place."

The Dowager's eyes narrowed just a little, making Marie fear that the lady would be able to ascertain the truth without her saying anything further.

"It was my fault," she said, making Marie frown. A sigh broke from her as she shook her head again. "I was the one who reminded the Duke about the heir, though I did not ever think that he would demand such a thing from you. I must beg your forgiveness in that, Marie."

"Forgiveness?" Mortified that her being bedded by her husband was now the topic of discussion, Marie tried to move the conversation on as quickly as she could. "I do not think there is anything for me to forgive, Your Grace."

"Calling me Helen will please me."

This made Marie smile, grateful that the Dowager had pulled down a barrier between them. Her kindness these last two weeks had been the only thing that had prevented Marie from sliding into complete blackness. "Helen.

As I was saying, I do not think there is anything for me to forgive. Your son did not injure me."

"Though with his words, he broke you."

This made Marie's smile shatter. "I..." Seeing the Dowager lift her eyebrow gently, she let out a small sigh. "I have found it difficult, indeed. The truth is, Helen, I have told your son that if I am not to be permitted to speak with him when I request a brief conversation, then I will keep him to such an ideal myself."

A look of understanding instantly leapt into the Dowager's eyes.

"That may well be wrong of me," Marie admitted, looking down at her tea rather than into the Dowager's face for fear that there would be accusation in the lady's gaze, "but I could not do anything else. There is so much anger directed at me, so much frustration that I did not feel able to open that door."

"I think you quite right to have done such a thing."

Relief seeped into Marie's heart as she finally looked back at her mother in law, seeing a small but sorrowful smile on the lady's face.

"He will have to learn one way or the other that he cannot treat you with such disdain. I would not expect you to permit him to do just as he pleases when he will not show you any sort of consideration."

Taking a sip of her tea, Marie hesitated for a second, then chose to ask her question. It had been something lingering on her mind for some time, though as yet she had not found the opportunity nor the courage to ask it. "You need not tell me but I have been wondering as to why the Duke has such an anger within him, why it is that he desires such a great and prolonged solitude."

The Duchess' eyebrows rose high. "You do not know?"

Marie shook her head.

"Martha has never told you?"

"No, she has not."

The Duchess' expression softened. "And you were good enough not to ask, though I am sure that your interest was piqued."

Feeling a little flustered, Marie sipped her tea before she answered. "I did not ever want to ask. Martha did mention that he was poor in spirit and that he disliked company because of some gathering of the past but I did not know anything else. And yes, I did not want to ask. It was not my place."

"But it is your place now." The Dowager smiled gently but Marie caught the slight hint of tears in her eyes. "My son was not always this way, I can assure you of that. It has been difficult to see him change into this dark, difficult man who does not want anything to do with any other."

Marie's heart pressed with sympathy though she did not say anything. She did not want to interrupt the Dowager, not when she had only just begun to explain.

"He was joyous, happy and contented," she continued, her shoulders rounding. "He was gentle and kind, especially with his sister. He was almost as excited as she for her come out!" Her eyes closed tightly. "But then, there was that one moment... that one incident where he took guilt upon himself and ruined his happiness."

Sipping her tea so that she would not begin to speak over the Dowager, Marie listened carefully, finding herself eager to know the gentleman she had married... or who it was he had once been.

"There was a house gathering." With another sigh, the Dowager clasped her hands tightly together, looking back at Marie. "My son was overjoyed, for his very dear friend, Lord Chesterton, became betrothed to the young lady he had been courting. Such was Lord Chesterton's exuberance, he imbibed a great deal and was very... merry, shall we say."

After saying this, the Duchess dropped her head and closed her eyes and Marie, immediately concerned, leaned forward and set her tea cup down. "Please, do not think that you need to speak if it is too difficult for you. I do not need to know in great detail."

At this, the Dowager looked up at her, her expression soft. "You are most considerate, Marie. Pray, do not think that I have no desire to share this with you, for I am more than willing to speak. It is only that I may find it a little difficult."

Still a little unsure that it would be wise for the lady to continue if it caused her such upset, Marie pressed her lips together and nodded, considering that if the lady continued to appear distressed, she would bring the conversation to a swift end, despite her own curiosity.

"As I was saying, Lord Chesterton was a little merry. The other gentlemen were to go hunting and Lord Chesterton, despite his imbibing, was most insistent that he attend with them. My son did his best to encourage him not to go but the man was determined. They had an argument in the stables but Lord Chesterton rode out with them on his horse, despite my son's warning."

"That was most unwise," Marie said, softly. "Not on the Duke's part, of course, but Lord Chesterton. Why would he be so foolish?"

"High spirits, mayhap?" The Duchess' smile was rueful. "The young ladies were all eager to celebrate together and thus, the gentlemen were to do the same. My son did his utmost to prevent Lord Chesterton from riding but I believe the man climbed on his horse and rode past him."

Marie shook her head. "But that was not the Duke's responsibility, was it?"

"No, it was not, as I have told him many a time. But it was not the horse riding that caused the difficulty, you understand." The Duchess' brows furrowed as she looked down at her clasped hands again, her voice breaking. "Lord Chesterton was not permitted to have a gun and my son was most insistent about that. However, somehow, he not only took a hold of one but also then rode back to where the gentlemen had just come from, seeming determined to shoot." Her voice wobbled and she came to a swift stop, a shaking breath escaping her. Marie wanted to say something, wanted to reassure her or to state that she need not continue, but the words would not come.

"Lord Chesterton rode through the forest near the manor house, all the way to a clearing where they had been shooting previously." The Duchess closed her eyes tightly, biting her lip for only a second before she finished. "Wessex and the other gentlemen went after him. Wessex rode through the forest on a different path, knowing it well and better than the others. Suddenly, as he was riding, he heard a gunshot."

Marie caught her breath, shock spreading like ice across her chest.

"Indeed," the Dowager murmured, looking back at Marie now. "When Wessex arrived, Lord Chesterton was gravely injured. Quite how he managed to shoot himself, I cannot think, but ever since that moment, ever since Wessex saw the injury caused, he blamed himself."

The air seemed thick and difficult to draw in as Marie fought to breathe steadily. Her eyes closed, her heart pounding as she imagined the difficulty the Duke had faced on that day.

"Lord Chesterton?" she asked, her voice thin. "Did he...?" She could not bring herself to say it, could not bring herself to ask that question but thankfully, the Dowager understood precisely what she was trying to say.

"It took a long time but yes, he recovered," she said, as Marie let out a rush of breath. "However, he still has a weakness in one of his legs and, much to his sorrow, his betrothed did not continue on with the engagement."

A mixture of sympathy and anger tore through Marie, making her close her eyes in an attempt to hide her reaction from the Dowager. How could a lady be so fickle as to turn her back on the gentleman she was supposed to care for? Surely an injury or an ongoing weakness would not be enough to drive one away?

"Lord Chesterton has written to my son on more than a few occasions but I know that he has never read any of his letters," the Dowager finished, hoarsely as a tear fell to her cheek. "I am also aware that Lord Chesterton does not blame the Duke for what happened, but Wessex will not listen to anything other than his own guilt."

"But why?" Marie asked, her own voice quavering a little. "Why will he refuse to listen? I cannot understand why, if his friend says there is no guilt to be held, he continues to cling to it."

The Dowager pressed her handkerchief to her cheek. "I cannot tell you, Marie," she said, brokenly. "At the beginning, when I noticed him retreating from company, I did try to speak with him. I asked him about what had happened, about why he was choosing to behave so but he did not answer me. Any time I tried to speak about Lord Chesterton, however, he threw my questions aside and hurried away, ending the conversation before it had even begun. It was then that I knew that guilt was tearing him apart."

"And it has continued to do so," Marie murmured, half to herself. "That is why he retreats from everyone, why he hides himself away. He does not want to speak of the guilt that weighs him down."

The Dowager nodded slowly. "Yes, but I also believe that he is almost afraid – though I do not mean to suggest he is weak in this – but afraid to have a close connection with anyone again, even with myself and his sister."

Not understanding this, Marie spread out her hands. "But why? Why would he push you both far from him? What good does that do?"

Again, a sad smile touched the Dowager's lips. "Because if he does not stay close to us, then nothing that he does – or does not do – will harm us."

Taking a few moments to consider, Marie nodded slowly. "So, by staying far from yourself and his sister, the Duke can be certain that nothing he decides will cause either of you harm."

"Precisely."

"But that is no way to live one's life!" Marie exclaimed, her heart filled with both compassion and a tiny hint of frustration that the Duke had chosen to punish himself in a way that was entirely unmerited. "He will have nothing but loneliness and pain for the rest of his days, should he continue."

The Dowager closed her eyes tightly, just as two tears slipped down onto her cheeks. "Indeed, he will," she agreed, ever so softly. "The truth is, Marie, I arranged this marriage for two reasons. One, because I was sure that you would be an excellent match for my son, able to give him all that he desired. Two – and I say this with regret and shame – because I hoped that you might be able to free him from this darkness."

Marie's eyes flared wide. "You think I will be able to help him in a way that Martha and you have not?" she asked, stunned. "As much as I wish that I could say with confidence that I will be able to, I am quite sure that I cannot! The Duke does not find my company in the least bit pleasing and all the stipulations that we both agreed to made it quite plain to me that he wants nothing more than to be left alone."

"I know, I know." The Dowager's tears were still coming but Marie did not move to go to sit with her and offer any comfort. She was still overcome with astonishment at what the Dowager had seemingly expected of her. "It was foolish and I will admit to that. You must understand, Marie, I am desperate to see my son return to who he once was! I have struggled to see him so sorrowful and so unwilling to spend even a *little* time with us, especially given that he once loved us so dearly."

I cannot hold anything against her for that.

Letting out a small sigh, Marie closed her eyes and let this new knowledge fill her. The Dowager was clearly distressed over the change in her son and Marie could not be angry with her for hoping that a marriage might change that. If she had found herself in such a situation where one of *her* siblings had altered entirely, where they had pushed her away over and over again, then would she not have tried anything to encourage them to return to who they had once been?

"I do not think I can do anything," she said, letting her hands spread out for a moment before putting them back in her lap. "The Duke will not even speak with me unless it is at a time when *he* desires it. If he will not change in that regard, then there can be no closeness between us."

"I know that and I certainly will not berate you for it," came the reply. "I am deeply concerned that I have set your feet onto a path that leads only to sadness and loneliness. For that, I am truly sorry."

"You have not." It was not exactly what Marie believed, for she was quite sure that her future did not have a good deal of happiness within it, but given the Dowager's brokenness, Marie could not say anything else. "Perhaps in time, things will change."

"Perhaps they will. Though, I have told my son that I intend to remain here a little longer before removing to the Dower House."

Appreciating the lady's concern, Marie smiled at her. "You need not do such a thing, Helen. You know how much I value your company but do not hold yourself back on my account."

"It is no trouble," the Dowager answered quickly as though she feared Marie would continue to rebuff her if she did not reassure her with all haste. "And I shall write to Martha to see when she can come to call. That way, she will be able to introduce you to the gentry nearby, for I am sure my son will not!"

Marie smiled. "I would very much like to see her again."

"Then I shall write this afternoon," the Dowager said. "I hope that, in some way, you will have some contentment in this household and in this marriage. Even if it is only a little."

"As do I," Marie answered, though she kept her voice low and quiet. "As do I."

Chapter Eleven

"That way, she will be able to introduce you to the gentry nearby, for I am sure that my son will not!"

Hearing his mother's words as they came drifting through the door towards him, Rupert stopped short, his brows knotting together. Rupert was fully aware that he was not exactly eager to be in company with his wife and therefore, all that had been said was quite true but all the same, it prodded him in a most frustrating manner.

"Then I shall write this afternoon," the Dowager said. "I hope that, in some way, you will have some contentment in this household and in this marriage. Even if it is only a little."

"Write?" Rupert said aloud, scowling. "To whom?"

He did not hesitate. Pushing open the door, he came directly into the room and stood tall. "Who will you be writing to, Mother?" he asked, crisply. "And who exactly will be bringing my wife some contentment?"

There was silence for a few seconds. Marie and the Dowager exchanged a look, only for both of them to rise to their feet and turn to face him directly.

"Good afternoon, Wessex," his mother said, smiling at him but with a hint of steel in her eyes. "I did not think that you would *ever* be so rude as to eavesdrop on a private conversation!"

Rupert's lip curled, hearing the rebuke in his mother's voice but refusing to respond to it. "This is my house, is it not? I can do whatever I please."

"It is also my house," his mother answered, quickly. "And it is Marie's also."

His wife lifted her gaze to his, a flush of color in her cheeks but her eyes clear. "It is my house too," she said, as if she needed to confirm that for herself. "However, if you are stating that it is quite all right for one to listen at the door to another's conversation, then I shall remember that." Her eyebrow lifted as he scowled darkly at her. "Recall that I shall be treating you in the very same manner as you treat me, Your Grace."

"Oh, you must call him Wessex!" the Duchess exclaimed, before Rupert could respond. "It is nonsense for a Duke's wife to refer to her husband in such terms."

"Wessex, then."

His mother chuckled, in spite of the conversation that had been going on between them. "If he is *most* trying, or if you are attempting to be a little affectionate – though quite why you would be, I cannot imagine – you may even try calling him Rupert. But have in mind that he does not like it when I do such a thing."

Marie laughed along with the Dowager, leaving Rupert in a state of angst. How dare his mother suggest such an impropriety? Indeed, a wife could refer to her husband in less formal terms but that was *only* at the request of her husband and certainly ought not to come from his own mother!

"Rupert." Marie said his name twice over, a small, light smile on her face. "I must say, Rupert does suit you very well, Wessex. Though I think I shall refer to you as Wessex from now on, given that you appear to be most displeased at my speaking either of those names!"

Everything that Rupert had been about to say died in an instant. Never before had Marie referred to him as either Wessex or Rupert but for some reason, the way that she spoke to him, the gentleness of her voice when she referred to him as such, stole all of his anger and upset away. He could not explain it. The fire that had burned hot and torn through him now faded to nothing. It had been doused completely, and all because she had spoken his name and smiled when she had said it.

"Wessex?"

Rupert cleared his throat, his hands balling into fists but not because of ire, rather because of his desire to regain a sense of control over himself. "Yes, Mother?"

"Are you truly stating that it is quite all right for us to eavesdrop on each other's conversations?" she asked, as embarrassment began a slow climb up Rupert's chest. "I am aware that you do not have very many acquaintances coming to call but that does not mean, surely, that you intend to permit us to stand outside your study door and listen to you as you go about your business and mutter away to yourself, is it?"

"Of course not," he snapped, struggling now to even glance in Lady Marie's direction. "That is not at *all* what I meant."

"Then what did you mean?" Marie asked, her expression open but with eyes that were slightly widened, as though pretending she was entirely innocent and did not know in the least bit what had upset him.

"I meant..." Rupert rubbed one hand over his face and growled low in his throat in exasperation. "Mother, I have told you many a time that I do not want you to invite anyone to this house without speaking to me first. I have only just had my sister's wedding breakfast and certainly do not want yet more guests!"

"Your sister's wedding was a little over two months ago!" The Dowager shook her head, a trilling laugh unsettling him all the more. "My goodness, you cannot think that to have a single visitor to the house would be an unpleasant situation, surely? Especially if it is only your sister."

"No." Rupert cut through the air with both hands. "No, she is not to be invited here. I will not have —"

"I will write to her today. Given that I am soon to remove to the Dower house, I think it is imperative that Marie is introduced to the gentry just as soon as possible."

Rupert sharpened his gaze. "Then you can do it."

The Dowager sighed and shook her head no. "You have no understanding of society any longer, it seems. Certainly, even though I might well be able to introduce Marie to some of the *ton,* it would be a good deal better for your sister to do so. I am acquainted with the older ladies, whilst Martha is acquainted with their daughters and the like. She is very dear friends with some of them and will be able to help a good deal better than I when it comes to your wife." She tilted her head, her eyes holding his gaze. "It is not as though you want Marie to be without friends, is it?"

Pulling his gaze away from his mother, Rupert returned it to his wife. Why did his heart slam hard in his chest when he looked into her green eyes? Most likely, he told himself, it came from a place of frustration. "I thought you preferred to read above all else," he said, tightly. "Why do you require friends?"

Marie's lips lifted just a little. "Because I am not like you," she said, but there was no trace of malice in her voice. "I do not prefer my own company to the company of others. Yes, I do prefer to read and to learn as much as I can, for that is one of the greatest joys of my life. While I am, at present, reorganizing the library, I would also prefer to have some friendships I can invest in also. Therefore, getting to know the families here is important to me. Besides which," she concluded, leaving Rupert very little room to argue, "I should very much like to see Martha again. I do miss her company a good deal."

The fight left him. Part of him wanted to refuse, to say that no, he could not let Martha come to call whilst the other part told him that it was pointless to argue. His mother would insist on writing to Martha, the letter would be sent even *without* his consent and no doubt, in a short time, his sister would arrive. He would not then only have his wife for company, he would have both his mother *and* his sister, which was the exact opposite of what he had always desired.

"She cannot stay for long," he bit out, as the Dowager beamed at him. "And Marie, *I* shall take you to meet the gentry. In fact, instead of that, I shall host a soiree to make sure you are acquainted with everyone, but only once Martha has arrived."

A stunned silence followed this statement and no one was more shocked than Rupert himself. He stared back at his wife as if *she* were responsible for him saying such a thing, despite knowing full well she was not. Why had he offered to do that for her? He did not want to spend time with anyone and he cared nothing for Marie herself, so why had he even suggested the soiree?

"You... you will host a soiree?"

Without a word, Rupert turned on his heel and strode from the room, leaving his wife's question unanswered. Slamming the door closed, he half ran, half walked back to his study, his chest burning as he dragged in air, his fingers pushing through his hair as confusion tore at him.

What have I done?

Closing the door to his study, Rupert strode across the room and picked up a brandy glass. Sloshing a good measure into it, he flung it back and then poured a second. It was only when he poured the third that he realized just how badly he was shaking.

Setting the glass down on the table, Rupert slumped down into a chair. Putting his head in his hands, he leaned forward, elbows on his knees and fingers gripping his hair.

Why? Why did I say such a thing?

Of course, he could retract his promise. he could straightforwardly acknowledge that he had erred and affirm he would do no such thing; yet, there was something within him that forbade it. He had observed the gleam of delight in his wife's eyes when he had spoken of the soirée, the astonishment that touched her lips, and the faint hope that lingered upon her countenance all the same.

He could not break that.

"This is because I feel guilty about attempting to bed her," he said aloud, his fingers slowly loosening from his hair as he squeezed his eyes closed. "That is all. How much of a fool I am!"

This was the one thing he did not want, the very thing he despised: company. To have these gentlemen and ladies present would remind him of the last time he had hosted such a gathering, of the time when Lord Chesterton had been here and when fate and his foolishness had led to such a dreadful scene. The very same had happened at Martha's wedding breakfast, though he had told no one. To have the guests, the noise of their conversation, the laughter and the music; all brought back the house gathering to his mind, over and over and *over* again until he had fought to even breathe steadily. This soiree, Rupert was sure, would be no different.

But there was nothing he could do. To take back what he had said would cause Marie a great deal of upset and he felt as though he had done enough of that already.

However, quite why he cared, Rupert could neither understand nor express and that made him deeply, deeply upset.

Chapter Twelve

"He is hosting a soiree for you?"

Marie nodded as Martha's eyes widened, her hand going to her heart.

"Are you quite sure?"

"As sure as I can be, given that I heard it from his lips – and your mother was present also, though I think she was just as astonished as I!"

"Goodness." Martha shook her head in astonishment, seeming not to know what else to say. They sat there in silence for some minutes as Marie sipped her tea and considered all that had taken place the last two weeks.

Ever since her husband had announced that he would hold a soiree for her to be introduced to the local gentry, he had all but practically disappeared. She barely saw him and the Dowager had, on more than one occasion, expressed concern for him for it was as if he had retreated all the more. He was now almost a ghost in the house, a specter that was very rarely seen and thereafter, spoken about in whispers for fear of disturbing him.

Marie had not known what to think. Though, then again, her thoughts had been very clouded indeed for she had a good many things to consider as regarded her husband. She had thought about all that she had learned of him, all that she had been told and her heart, rather than turning against him, had warmed with sympathy and compassion. It was very strange to feel such a way for a gentleman that she did not know very well at all but all the same, the thoughts lingered, as did her ever increasing concern. He was a gentleman who had shown her nothing but disregard and, at times, callousness but that did not mean that she was to reject him. Part of her was beginning to wonder just what the Duke might be like if he were to not only forgive himself for the past but realize that the guilt he had shouldered for so long was not his burden to bear.

"Marie?"

"Mmm?" Realizing she had been lost in thought, she offered Martha a slightly apologetic smile. "Forgive me, I was thinking about the soiree and all that is to be offered to me."

Martha smiled gently, her eyes holding to Marie's. "It must be very exciting for you. You have done very well being wed to my brother, I must say."

Marie laughed softly. "We are less than three months wed and, truth be told, I have barely set eyes on him!" Her smile faded as she recalled how he had tried to enter her bedchamber and how, thereafter, she had been forced to stand against his anger. That, at least, had not been something he had tried again. Perhaps he understood that she was not about to give in and, much to his credit, he was not about to take his right by force.

"You are worried about it all?"

With a slightly wry smile and a little embarrassed that her thoughts had shown so clearly in her expression, Marie spread out her hands. "It is concerning to me, indeed."

"Because you are unacquainted with the gentry?"

"Because your brother, I am sure, did not mean to suggest he would throw a soiree," Marie answered, with a small sigh. "I saw him when he spoke those words. It was as if he had astonished himself as much as your mother and myself! There was no opportunity for him to take those words back either, for your mother exclaimed aloud and then all was set in stone!"

"And he has since retreated entirely, so I hear," Martha added, as Marie nodded. "My mother informed that she has seen him only a handful of times since then and has never been able to have a discussion with him about it all."

Marie nodded, her hands back in her lap. "Indeed."

"You will have been relieved not to have seen him, I am sure." Martha's lips lifted just a little. "How are things, might I ask? I know it is a bold question but I must ask."

Unsure as to what to say, Marie hesitated, then closed her eyes. "In truth, Martha, it has been difficult." When she opened her eyes, her friend was smiling sympathetically. "I did not realise that he intended to only speak with me when *he* desired it, rather than permitting me to be the one to speak with him whenever I wished."

Martha's smile fell away.

"However, I have made it quite clear that whatever standards he holds for me, I will return to him," Marie continued, with a shrug. "That means, if I must wait until *he* is ready to speak with me about any matter – or anything that *I* would like to speak about – then I shall hold him to the same. I will not speak with him unless I have decided it is something I wish to do."

"Goodness." Martha's lip curved. "I presume this has not been taken with any sort of delight."

This made Marie chuckle wryly. "Indeed, it has not. However, there is nothing to be done. I am determined and he is quickly learning that I will not turn away from what I desire. Though," she finished, a little heavily, "I have been told in detail as to *why* the Duke acts as he does. That is something I am sorry for."

Martha's expression quickly clouded. "It is most dreadful. All he has to do is to accept that he holds no guilt upon his shoulders and all will be well! If he had done so at the beginning, then I am sure he would still be the brother that I knew him to be. He would not be hiding away, would not be retreating into the shadows."

Considering this, Marie nodded slowly. "And Lord Chesterton's letters have remained unread?"

"They have not been opened, from what I understand," Martha answered, with a shake of her head. "My brother did not speak of it but I confess to having one of the maids confirm that detail with me, so I might be certain."

"But if only he would read one, then he might realise there is nothing to be gained from holding onto such guilt!"

Before Martha could respond, the door opened and the Duke came in directly, though he did not look at Marie. The atmosphere instantly changed as if heavy clouds, full of thunder and terror, had come over them, leaving Marie's stomach in tight knots.

"Martha. I had heard you had arrived." The Duke inclined his head to his sister, his expression unchanging. "You will be able to provide Marie with some excellent company, I am sure."

"I shall, especially since you are unwilling to do such a thing," came the clear, sharp reply, making Marie's breath hitch. "You are missing out on a good many excellent conversations, brother."

The Duke snorted and turned on his heel, barely even acknowledging Marie though when their eyes caught for only a moment, a shiver ran straight down her spine. "I hardly think so."

"That does not speak very well of your wife, does it?" Martha rose to her feet suddenly, striding after her brother. "You need not be so disrespectful, Wessex. It is not kind."

But he is not kind, Marie thought to herself, heavily, keeping her gaze away from both brother and sister. *I wonder if he has ever been so.*

"I was just telling Marie that you were never so before," she heard Martha say, the knot in her stomach tightening painfully now. "You were always thoughtful, considerate and generous, both with your time and your attention. Now, to see you so rude and disinclined towards the wonderful lady who is your wife quite breaks my heart."

The Duke turned to face his sister, though Marie kept her gaze away from him, looking studiously at the fireplace as though somehow, it was the most beautiful fireplace she had ever seen.

"I would prefer it if you would not speak of me to anyone," he grated, angrily. "Not even to my wife."

Martha laughed harshly. "I am sure that your wife would prefer a good many things but you are so utterly selfish that you will not even give her a single thought!"

Marie winced, then got to her feet, turning to face them both. "Please, Martha, you need not defend me. I am quite contented, truly."

"You are not." Martha shook her head, then pointed one finger at her brother. "You may be throwing a soiree but that does not mean your wife is contented and happy with your relationship."

"She knew what she was to have in this marriage," came the fiery response, as though she was not even standing there, listening to them both. "You speak too openly, Martha! Can you not keep your thoughts to yourself?"

"There is no need –"

Marie's attempt to placate them both was brought to a sharp end by Martha's furious interruption.

"I *can* keep my thoughts to myself but I am choosing not to do so, given just how coldly you treat Marie! She is my dear friend and one of the most remarkable ladies I have known. Why do you not step out from the shadows of the past and into the light of your future? Why must you cling to your guilt and –"

"Enough!" The Duke's roar seemed to shake the very ceiling, cutting through the air with one hand, silencing his sister. "You are *not* to speak of that, Martha. Not to anyone. And especially not to *her*."

Marie's whole body trembled. She wanted to open her mouth and tell him that she was already aware of all that had taken place, of all that he had endured but she could not. Not when he was this vehemently angry. In only a breath, in only a single moment, he had changed and railed at his sister, clearly desiring to keep all that she knew of the past to herself.

And yet, Marie knew it all already.

The Duke threw her a look – there was something in his look that Marie could not make out – and then hurried from the room. The slamming of the door behind him made Marie tremble again, but Martha only rolled her eyes, let out an exclamation and then slumped back into her chair.

"He never used to be in such tempers," she said, waving a hand as Marie slowly sank back down into her chair. "This is only because I have done or said something that has brought back his memory of the past. Clearly, he is just as upset about it all as he has ever been."

"Do... do you think that I should tell him?"

Martha looked back at her, then sat up straighter in her chair, her eyes widening a little. "My dear friend, you are not worried about speaking with him, are you?"

A little unsure how to answer, for she did not want to speak unfairly about the Duke, Marie took a few moments to respond. When she did, it was with slow, careful words that she hoped portrayed her concern without speaking falsehoods about him.

"I would admit to being concerned, indeed," she said, as Martha listened without interruption. "As I have already told you, the Duke has no interest in speaking with me about anything, has no desire for me to be in his company in any way or at any time. I cannot imagine what he would say – or do – if I told him that I already knew of Lord Chesterton and all that had taken place."

"Do?" Martha's eyes rounded. "My goodness, Marie! Are you saying that my brother has been cruel to you? That he has... *hurt* you?"

"No, no, not at all," Marie replied, hastily, as Martha's eyes closed in clear relief. "However, if I am to be honest... and believe me, I say this without any intention of showing disrespect – that I am a trifle afraid that he might be cruel, were I to upset him to any great extent."

"I see." Martha murmured, sinking into her chair with a composed yet subdued air. Her countenance had grown noticeably paler, yet she regarded Marie intently, a silence lingering between them before she spoke again.

"Well, what I can say to that is that I have never known my brother to lift a finger against anyone. He was always considerate, willing to help even an animal when it was injured or in pain. Do you know that, rather than shooting one of the sheep from the local tenant who had injured its leg, he sent the veterinary surgeon to it?" Her lips quirked. "I do not know whether the tenant or the sheep was more surprised, but my brother knew just how much that ram meant to his tenant."

This did not sound in any way like the Duke, Marie considered, her heart aching for the gentleman he had once been.

"The veterinary surgeon did as my brother asked, of course, given that he was the Duke," Martha continued, with a faraway look coming into her eyes. "He was paid substantially too, with the tenant paying not even a single coin."

"That sounds vastly different from the gentleman I know," Marie said, speaking her thoughts aloud and hoping that it would not upset her friend to say such things. "I do wish that he had not changed so. I think... well, I know that things would be vastly different even between us, were he not so burdened."

"You might well have fallen in love with him," Martha sighed, with a shake of her head. "He was a very popular gentleman in London, as you can imagine, given his standing, his fortune and his good heart. But he told me once he would never marry a young lady simply because she desired his wealth and standing." She began to blink quickly, pushing back the tears that Marie caught glistening there. "I think you would have done very well together, truth be told."

Marie nodded but said nothing, trying to imagine what it would have been like to have had the Duke as her husband as he had been, not as he was now. Indeed, she considered, she might very well have developed an affection for him, given the kind of generous heart he so clearly had once had. Her eyes closed tightly, a sudden knot in her throat though she tried her best not to show this to her friend. Martha did not need to know her pain or her struggle. It was her own to bear, a burden she had taken on willingly and she could not turn back from it now.

All the same, she thought to herself, her heart heavy in her chest, *I do wish that I had known him before all of this.* A small flicker of hope began to burn in her heart, but Marie quickly fought to extinguish it. All the same, it would not do as she demanded, continuing to burn despite her attempts to rid herself of it. The thought lingered, tying itself to her heart.

Perhaps, just perhaps, there might be that very same gentleman still hiding there... and one day, somehow, he might return.

All she could do was hope.

Chapter Thirteen

"Brother?"

Rupert groaned aloud, closed his eyes and flung his head back against his seat.

"I care nothing for your whining," his sister said, marching into the study as though she had every right to be present. "I must speak with you."

"Martha, you have been here for a little less than a day and you are already insisting upon interrupting me," Rupert said, sitting up properly and scowling at his sister, even if that made very little difference. "I have already told you, I require solitude and –"

"And I will not be held back by your selfishness," she interrupted, loudly, "for that is what this is. Nothing but selfishness, Wessex."

Rupert shrugged. "I do not care."

"You should. Can you not see the damage this does to us all? Your silence, your coldness, your absence makes Mama, Marie and I all upset and troubled."

With a roll of his eyes, Rupert let out as heavy a sigh as he could muster. "Marie signed an agreement, giving her the stipulations required for this marriage. She knew that I was not going to be a husband present with her."

"And you still think that to live such a way is a good thing?"

"I am contented with it." As he said those words, Rupert's conscience bit down hard upon him but he did his best to ignore it. That in itself was not true. He was not in the least bit contented. The last two weeks, ever since he had stated that he would host a soiree for Marie, he had been nothing but distracted and confused. When he awoke in the morning, his first thought had been of her. Somehow, the image of her wide-eyed expression, her mouth a circle of surprise and astonishment dancing in her green eyes had been the only thing in his thoughts. He had not known why she lingered there, had not understood her presence and yet, with every effort to remove her, she only lingered all the more. Thus, he had removed himself from her company all the more, barely seeing her more than once or twice every few days... but that had, to his great frustration, done very little also.

"Do you know that she is afraid of you?"

The quietness in Martha's voice made Rupert's eyebrows lift, his heart suddenly squeezing with a cold feeling he did not understand. "Afraid?"

"Yes," she said, plainly. "She is afraid of you."

"What do you mean?" This made Rupert sit up straight, his eyes fixed to Martha's, both a little concerned about what she had said and yet, silently hoping that she was lying solely to get his attention.

"You came to interrupt us, as you might recall," she said, taking a seat instead of standing in front of his desk. "You came to greet me, though I cannot say that there was much of a greeting there!"

Rupert scowled. "Do you mean only to come here and berate me?"

"Yes." Her eyebrow lifted as though to remind him that she was just as determined as he, making Rupert grit his teeth, hard. His sister had, over the last two years, been persistent in her attempts to have him speak with her, to engage with both herself and her mother and he had grown tired of it. To have her now returned, albeit for a short while, was rapidly stealing his energy from him.

"As I was saying," Martha continued, crisply, "you came to greet me but there was practically no warmth in your words or your welcome which, I will tell you, did injure me."

Rupert's heart twisted but he did not say a word.

"Thereafter, when we were in discussion about your manner towards your wife, you spoke very sharply to me when I was about to mention Lord Chesterton."

Recalling this, Rupert gripped both hands together, refusing to let himself react to her words, as he had done before. Indeed, he was well able to admit that he had not only responded badly when he had spoken with both Martha and Marie earlier that day, but he had also stormed out of the room and slammed the door so hard, the handle had rattled.

Still, after all this time, he could not let anyone so much as mention Lord Chesterton without fear and guilt tearing at his soul.

"Once you had quit the room, in the manner you did, Marie and I had a small conversation," his sister continued, as Rupert fought to keep his breathing steady. "It turns out, *dear* brother, that she is afraid that you may physically injure her at some juncture."

All of Rupert's breath left his body as he stared back into his sister's angry face, seeing the fury lighting her eyes and the color in her cheeks. Never had he thought that his wife would think such a thing as that!

"She is afraid that, should she say something that would anger you, your fury would be so great that it would strike her in some manner or other," Martha finished, leaning forward in her chair. "I reassured her that you were not that sort of gentleman and that even though your character has altered completely, you are not the sort of fellow who would ever injure her in that way."

"No, no, I would not," Rupert said, emphatically, but his voice lacked any sort of energy or strength. "I do not know why she would think such a thing. I..." His response faded away, his gaze drifting from his sister as he recalled just how angry he had been when she had blocked him from her bedchamber. Had he not near enough thrown himself at the door in an attempt to break through it? Had he not threatened her in such a way as to shake her with fear, all in the hope that she would do as he asked?

"Wessex?"

He looked back at his sister. "I would not harm her," he rasped, praying that she believed him. "I would never put one hand upon her."

"I know that," she said, gently. "But consider, brother, just how much your attitude, your behaviour and your manner towards your wife is damaging her. If you want any sort of connection with her, however small, you cannot continue to treat her with such callousness, Wessex. Do you want her to continue to believe that she is in danger from your hand?"

Shaking his head, Rupert ran one hand over his face.

"Then do something about it," Martha said, her tone quite matter of fact as she rose to her feet. "I hope to see you at dinner."

"Wait, Martha." Rupert was half out of his chair before she had made her way to the door. "What am I to do?"

A look of surprise etched itself into her expression and she did not respond for some moments. When she did, it was with a softness about her eyes and a tenderness in her smile that spoke of sympathy, though Rupert felt his heart hardening against it. He did not deserve any sort of kindness.

"Why not just speak with her?" she suggested, quietly. "Why not just tell her that you will not harm her, perhaps apologise for some of your harshness?" Her shoulders lifted and then fell. "All you can do is talk, Wessex. Try that."

It felt almost an insurmountable challenge given all that Rupert had just learned. His mouth went dry, his thoughts spiraling as he fought to think of what he might even *begin* to say to the lady. When he finally had found some sort of clarity, he returned his gaze to his sister to ask her what she might suggest by way of even starting such a conversation but she was already gone.

Sitting down heavily, Rupert planted both elbows on the desk and shoved his fingers into his hair.

I do not want her to think that I will do anything to harm her, he told himself, firmly. *That is my focus, my only consideration. And somehow, I will do it.*

***

"Marie?"

The swift intake of breath and the way she took a step or two back told Rupert that not only had he surprised her by his presence, but he was not entirely welcome either.

"I am sorry," he continued, holding up both hands. "I do not mean to interrupt you, especially when it is late but I wondered if you might spare me a moment."

The lady, who was now clutching a book to her chest as though it was some sort of defense against him, a shield which she held in place, gave him only a tiny nod.

"I thank you." Coming a little further into the room, Rupert became aware of how her gaze fastened on him, although she did not look into his eyes. It was as if she were attempting to make certain of his presence at every turn.

He despised himself all the more for what his anger had, albeit unwittingly, done.

"I wanted to reassure you," he said, stumbling over his words a little. "To reassure you that I do not mean you any harm."

"Harm?" It was the first word she had spoken, but it held surprise. "What do you mean?"

Rupert closed his eyes, then turned away so he did not have to look at her. "The evening that I came to you, the evening that you had blocked the door from me... I know that I did not react well. I did not respond with any sort of understanding or kindness, did I?"

"No," she agreed, surprising him by her firm response. "You most certainly did not."

Turning back towards her, Rupert spread out both hands either side and then let them fall. "I know that I did not speak to you with gentleness and my physical response must have been a little frightening. I know... I know how you were discovered the following morning and I can only imagine that it was because of what you had endured the previous evening." A knot came into his throat as he spoke and when he dared to look into her face, he felt nothing but shame pour over him. Burning heat went from the top of his head to his toes as he saw the glistening tears in her eyes, hating himself for the pain and fright he had caused her.

"Please." An urgency pushed him closer to her and much to his relief, she did not rush back. "Please understand, Marie, I would never have forced myself upon you. I would never have physically injured you in order to get what I believed was my right to take. That is not the sort of gentleman I am."

"No?"

The doubt in her face made his eyes close, his breathing rasping. "No," he said, heavily, "though I can well understand why you would think otherwise." When he opened his eyes, she was looking back at him with slightly widened eyes, but there was no fear that he could see and that was something of a relief.

"Martha told me that you were not such a character," she said, after a time. "I can do my best to trust you in this, Wessex."

His throat constricted and he could only nod. There were so many emotions swirling through him that he could barely breathe, trying to keep his head above the water. For some reason, he could not seem to pull his gaze from hers, as though looking into her eyes was the only way to keep from drowning.

She was watchful now, searching his face perhaps to discover if there was something there that whispered of lies.

"I want you to trust me in this," he managed to say, eventually. "Even if you trust me in nothing else."

Her smile was sad. "If only there was not so much anger in you, then it might be easier for me to believe such a thing about you."

Rupert nodded, accepting this but finding no response to give her. He was all too aware of his anger but felt as though he could do nothing with it. It was a part of him now, borne from that incident two years ago where he had been solely responsible for Lord Chesterton's accident. An accident that had cost him so much.

"Thank you for coming to speak with me." She looked down at her book, now cradling it in her arms rather than holding it close to her. "I need you to know something."

"Oh?" There was something about her that was pulling him to her, he could tell. Trying to set it aside, aware that this was the first conversation they had ever shared together, Rupert looked away from her eyes, fearing that the vividness of them was what was pulling him in. "What is it?"

She hesitated.

"I will not become angry," he promised, telling himself inwardly that even if he did feel such a thing, he would contain himself in any way he knew how. "I can assure you of that."

She looked down at her hands. "It is only to say that I know everything."

"Everything?" Rupert frowned, not certain what she meant. "You speak of – of..." His eyes closed, the mortification that had only just left him beginning to tear through him again. "My sister, no doubt."

"Your mother, in fact."

And how little she must think of me now. If I was not already low in her estimation, how much further have I fallen!

"I am sorry for it all."

This was not the response he had expected and he turned his head to look straight at her, surprise shooting through him and making his breath hitch.

"You will not want me to say this, I am sure, but I shall say it anyway since I have opportunity." The breath she took in was a little tremulous but she lifted her chin just a little. "I do not think you responsible and I think it a great pity that you have such a burden of guilt on your shoulders, one that you yourself refuse to set aside." With another breath, she closed her eyes. "Martha told me of the sort of gentleman you once were. How many things might change if only you would set down this weight!"

Rupert's jaw tightened, his heart twisting painfully. He could not talk about this, could not share with her the pain that caught him every time he thought about Lord Chesterton and that dreadful day. He could not tell her of the nightmares that haunted him some nights, reminding him of all that had happened, nor could he tell her of the fear that he would make a foolish decision again, should he let himself get close to her – or to anyone else.

"It is not something you wish to speak of, I understand."

"No, it is not."

Her lips pressed tightly together but she did not step away from him, despite the quick and somewhat sharp response. "Then I shall not." She licked her lips. "I thank you for holding back your anger. It is appreciated, Rupert."

It was as though a bolt of lightning had struck him. Everything in him went ablaze all at once, leaving him burning with heat. He could not breathe, could only stare down into her face, his mind blank but his heart thundering within him. Concern flickered in her eyes, a slight lowering of her brows telling him that she was confused by this strange reaction – and still, he could neither move nor speak.

"Are you quite well?" She came a little closer to him and the sweet scent of honey ran lightly through his nostrils, sending yet more fire into his veins. "Wessex, are you -?"

When her hand touched his, Rupert came alive at once. Pulling back from her, wheeling around, he practically ran to the door. Without another word, he opened it and threw himself from the room, terrified by what it was he felt and what it might mean.

Heart pounding, sweat pouring down his back, he rushed back to his study without so much as a glance in any other direction. The door closed, he poured himself a glass of whiskey and threw it back... and then took another, and another.

In time, the feelings began to fade, dulled by the liquor now flowing through his veins. His heart slowed, his eyes grew tired, his body sluggish. Sitting down, decanter in one hand and glass in the other, Rupert did not stop until every single flicker of emotion was gone from him, drowned by all he had imbibed.

The decanter slid from his hand, his eyes closed and he slumped back into his chair until blackness took him.

Chapter Fourteen

"Drunk, I tell you! The footmen found him in the study this morning."

Marie frowned, hesitating as she stopped at the door to her bedchamber, hearing the two maids gossiping with each other just inside.

"The Duke is never merry," the second maid said. "Seems strange to me that he would do that."

"I know, it is very strange indeed! Especially since we all heard him say he would never let himself become intoxicated again, not after Lord Chesterton."

Marie's eyebrows lifted. The Duke had become drunk last evening? She had wondered at his strange reaction to her hand touching his, had seen him rushing from the room and had gone after him, concerned for him in her own way but he had already been gone by the time she had reached the door. He had chosen to drink himself to slumber, then? That did seem very strange. With a clearing of her throat to alert the maids to her presence, she pushed open the door to her bedchamber and stepped inside. Two red faced maids met her, bobbing curtsies as she made her way through to her dressing table.

"I think something more than a chignon is required," she said, addressing her lady's maid. "A little more elegant, since I am to go to the village." She eyed her lady's maid as she came closer, ready to help Marie with her hairstyle for the day. "I should like it if you did not whisper about my husband."

"Of course, Your Grace," the maid whispered, looking more than a little ashamed. "I am sorry, we did not think that you were – that is, we shouldn't have been doing that. I'm terribly sorry."

"As am I." The other maid bobbed another curtsy and then hurried from the room, leaving Marie alone with her lady's maid. She smiled gently, hoping to relieve the maid's worry a little.

"It is the natural way of things, I know," she said, as the maid began to unpin her hair, letting it fall to its natural length. "But one must be very careful what is said about the Duke. It would not be good for you to be overheard and then lose your position because of it, would it, Betty?"

"No, Your Grace."

"And I should be very displeased if I were to lose you," Marie finished, seeing the small smile dart across the maid's face. "You are an excellent lady's maid and I do not think I will be able to find another as good and as kind as you."

The maid's face flushed. "Thank you, Your Grace. You are very kind."

"My wife, where is she?"

Marie caught her breath, hearing the Duke's loud voice coming through from the hallway. Shooing her maid into the dressing room so she might close the door and be away from whatever was to take place, Marie made her way to the door and then opened it, only to come face to face with the Duke.

He was white faced, with red rimmed eyes that gazed down at her. One hand reached out, grasping first her shoulder, then sliding down her arm to her hand.

"What have you done to me?" he rasped, his eyes wide as he pressed her hand not too gently. "I do not want this, Marie. I want nothing but to keep you away from me!"

Not understanding in the least, Marie gazed back at him, her breath catching in her throat. "I do not know what you mean, Rupert."

His eyes squeezed closed. "You cannot call me that. You must not!"

She did not know what to say to that, not understanding him in the least. He was like a whirlwind, furious and terrible, upending all that she felt.

"Why are you so...?"

The question was not one that she understood, nor one that she could answer. Gazing back into his eyes, she saw them still wide and staring, his face still as pale as it had been when he had first thrown himself into her room.

"I do not understand." Looking into his eyes, she tried to keep her voice as calm and as steady as she could, speaking honestly and reminding herself of all that had been shared between them the previous evening. He had come to reassure her that he would never physically harm her and had even apologized, in a way, for his actions prior to that. She knew more about him now, did she not? She understood him a *little* better, though at this moment, Marie felt herself as lost as ever! Frowning gently, she took a step closer to him, just as the Duke pushed both hands through his hair.

"Wessex, if there is something I am doing that is troubling you, then all you need to do is share it with me," she said, as calmly as she could. "That is all I ask of you. I do not want to upset you, truly." Taking a step closer, she put one hand out to him but he drew back as though she was offering him fire. "Please, just tell me what it is."

"You." The Duke groaned, scrubbed one hand over his face and turned away from her. "The problem is *you*, Marie."

Her heart roared, then began to pour sadness into her. "What do you mean?" she asked, hurrying after him, coming out into the hallway as the other servants faded away into the shadows, clearly aware that the Duke was in some sort of ill temper. "Rupert, please wait!"

He rounded on her then, his face flushed hot instead of pale white. "I have told you *not* to call me that!"

Coming to a stop only a step away from him, Marie lifted her chin, reminding herself that he had promised never to put a finger on her. "And yet, I am determined to hold you to the same standards as you hold me to. If you call me Marie, then I have every right to call you Rupert, do I not?"

Something like pain tore through the Duke's expression and seeing it, Marie's heart instantly softened. There was something in this that she did not understand, something that she simply could not get any sort of bearing on but regardless, it was causing the Duke some sort of tremendous agony.

"You have already suffered a great deal," she said, softly, staying exactly where she was. "I do not want to add to your torment, truly. You must tell me *why* I cannot call you Rupert, why I am such a problem to you, else I cannot understand."

"And must you truly understand in order to do as I ask?"

She nodded yes, though this only made the Duke groan aloud, as though she had said something truly frustrating. Again, the knot of worry and twists of fear began to tighten in her core but Marie did not give them any consideration. It was as though she were beginning to see the truth about the Duke's dark demeanor, his anger and his ire.

He was afraid.

"I want to understand," she said, as gently as she could. "We are husband and wife, are we not? Yes, you and I agreed it was near enough in name only but that does not mean you cannot share anything with me, especially if you are demanding I do not refer to you in a particular way." Seeing the way his shoulders began to lower, Marie took a tiny step forward. "All you need to do is explain. I will not disagree or argue. All I want to do is understand."

The Duke lowered his head, closed his eyes and then let out a low groan that sounded, to Marie's ears, as though he were in some sort of agony that could not be expressed.

"I did not want this," he rasped, not lifting his gaze to hers. "This is not at all what I wanted."

"I do not understand what you mean," Marie answered, relieved that he was not roaring at her now. "What is it that frightens you so?"

He did not state, in an instant, that he was not afraid of anything, nor did his head snap up as he berated her for her curiosity. Instead, he let out another sound, followed by a long breath that seemed to drain him, given the way his shoulders and back rounded.

"I did not want *this*," he said, again, as though somehow she would understand. "When you call me Rupert, my heart... it responds in a manner that I do not like."

Marie's breath hitched, her chest becoming tight and painful as the Duke slowly lifted his head and looked back into her eyes.

"I hate it," he said, as she fought to breathe. "I want it gone from me, Marie. I cannot have this."

"Why... why not?" she managed to say, her heartbeat beginning to grow quicker now as her mind took a full hold of what it was he had been trying to express. "Why can you not permit your heart to do all that it wishes?"

When his eyes finally found hers, they were filled with such shadows, it was as if every bit of blue had been drained from them. His shoulders hunched, his expression haunted, he looked back at her with pain pouring into his gaze.

"I deserve no happiness," he said, hoarsely. "I cannot and will not ever be close to anyone again – not to my mother, to my sister nor to you. I have already caused a lifetime of suffering for a friend. I will not let that happen again."

Marie's heart broke into a thousand pieces.

"Please, only call me Wessex," he said, putting out one hand to her, but it was with his palm out to her, as if he was seeking to prevent her from speaking his Christian name again. "And do not come to seek me out. I cannot bear it." Upon saying this, he turned and made his way from her, leaving Marie to stand alone in the hallway, her very self seeming to shatter. She had never understood her husband, had never once come to any sort of understanding as to why he was so despondent and selfish. Now, however, she *finally* saw the truth for what it was.

Fear drove him. Fear that tore through him and told him that he could never step into close relationship with anyone for fear that he would do as much damage to them as he had supposedly done to Lord Chesterton.

And if only he would, then I might find that the gentleman I have married is just as Martha described him to be, Marie thought to herself, her eyes closing as she felt dampness on her cheeks. If he forgave himself, if he released the burden he had been carrying for so long, then would he not return to the gentleman that Martha and the Dowager had described, the one they missed desperately?

And would it not also permit him to let himself feel everything within his heart? If he did, then what would that mean for her? For them both?

Turning away, Marie made her way slowly back to her own bedchamber, both overcome and sorrowful from the conversation with her husband. The tiny flickering hope still burned on in her heart but she felt it now smaller than ever before. If he would not let himself step away from the past, then what hope could she truly have?

"I do not know what to do," she murmured to herself, closing the door of her bedchamber and going to sit down at the dressing table again, expecting the maid to arrive very soon. With all of her book learning, she had never once read anything that could tell her what to do in this present circumstance. Closing her eyes, she let the tears fall, fully aware that she was nothing but a jumbled mess of confusion when it came to the Duke of Wessex.

Just what was she to do?

Chapter Fifteen

One week later.

"I am in agony." Rupert gazed back at his reflection, despising everything that he saw. It had been a sennight since he had woken up in his study, his dreams having been nothing but his wife, his mind full of thoughts of her. One week since he had gone to her rooms to tell her that she could not come near him, could not call him 'Rupert' and most certainly could not linger in his company in any way. He had thought it would bring him relief, would give him a sense of calmness and help to restore his mind and heart… but it had not.

Instead, all he had been able to do was think of her.

It had been both disconcerting and deeply upsetting, for Rupert had not wanted to have a single thought trace back to her and instead, his mind had been flooded with Marie. Her eyes, so vivid and her smile – only once or twice directed towards him. He had found himself yearning for her to smile upon him once more, for a radiant spark to ignite within her eyes as she gazed up at him.

And then, he had hated himself for even thinking such a thing. That was what had driven him to go to her, to speak with her and to demand that she should stay back from him and never call him Rupert again. What he had not expected was to be met with a beautiful creature whose hair was streaming down from both shoulders, free and dancing lightly with every step she had taken towards him. It had been as though someone had punched him hard in the stomach, stealing both breath and sense as he had looked at her and found himself lost. She did not know that she had added to his torture, of course, but he had not been able even to allow her close to him. He had explained himself as best he could, though that had not been with particularly coherent sentences given the state of his heart and mind.

Then, he had retreated completely. It was the only thing he had thought to do but it had brought him no peace.

Now, one sennight later, it was time for the soiree and Rupert wanted nothing more than to hide away. He had berated himself almost every hour as the time had approached, had delegated a good deal of the organizing to his mother so he would not have to think on it as though, somehow, that would prevent it from happening.

It had not, of course, and now he was to spend the evening in fine company, wishing that he were not present. It was one thing to be in amongst the gentry but quite another to have his wife by his side, as would be expected. Quite how he was to be near her for so long without losing his mind, Rupert did not know.

"Might I come in?"

A knock and the voice at the door told Rupert it was his mother. Gritting his teeth to keep his frustration at bay, he looked down at the floor. No doubt, she would have something to say about this evening, or about his ill manner this last week or mayhap about Marie and he did not want to hear any of it.

"I will not say a word of complaint or rebuke, if that is what concerns you," she said, her voice penetrating through the door as though, somehow, she had heard him think such a thing. "I promise you that."

Knowing that he could not simply hide himself away and pretend that she was not there, Rupert glared back at his reflection as if somehow, permitting her entry was a weakness. "If you must, Mother."

"I must," she said, opening the door at once and stepping in. "Ah, you *are* dressed, that is a relief, at least."

"You did not think that I would be neglectful of my duties, did you?" Her silence made his eyebrows lift, his heart twisting as he turned to face her. "You thought I might stay back from it all?"

His mother spread out her hands. "You did assign Martha's responsibilities to me, Wessex. I did wonder if you would do the very same with this."

Shame began to flicker in Rupert's chest, threatening to, very quickly, become a torrent that would wash over him. Indeed, he *had* told his mother that if Martha wanted a come out, she would have to do it for he was not going to set foot in London but that had not been out of selfishness. It had come from a place of deep upset, where he did not think he would be able to even *think* about facing society.

"However, I understand why you did so, just as I can understand why you might shirk from this," she continued, again making Rupert think that somehow, she was able to read all that was in his thoughts. "In truth I was hopeful that you would not shy away from this soiree. I know it means a great deal to Marie."

Rupert looked away, scowling. "I am dressed, as you can see. Is that why you came? You wished to make certain that I was prepared for the soiree?"

"No, that was not my purpose in my coming." His mother's eyes searched his and she came a little closer to him. "Is all well?"

"Well?" Rupert repeated, confused. "I do not know what you mean."

"You have hidden yourself away a good deal more than I have ever seen you," she said, by way of explanation. "And Marie... well, she is a little altered also."

"Altered?" At this, Rupert's heart lurched though he quietened it hastily. "What do you mean?"

The Dowager's lips twisted. "She is always so very deep in thought, barely listens to anything that is said and when I try to bring her back into the conversation, she apologises and does attempt to listen before fading into herself again."

Rupert shrugged, trying to ignore the stab of concern he felt. "I am sure she is only thinking about something she has read recently, something that has caught her attention."

"Oh, no, it cannot be that, for she has never once picked up a book these last seven days!" The Dowager bit her lip, looking away. "I do not know what to make of it, truth be told, for I do not know her well enough to ask her directly and Martha states that all is well."

Rupert sighed heavily, in an attempt to tell his mother that this conversation was a waste of his time whilst inwardly beginning to worry. "If Martha says all is well, then I would trust her. She knows Marie better than you or I and therefore –"

"And what a great pity that is," his mother interrupted, with a small sigh of her own. "I would have thought that you, as her husband, would have known the lady better than Martha or myself and yet, here I am coming to tell you about your wife's change in character."

His scowl deepened. "I thought you were doing your utmost not to criticise me, Mother."

"It is not a criticism, more just a statement," she answered, turning away from him. "I am glad to see that you are ready for the soiree. Come and join us soon, Wessex. The guests will soon arrive and your wife will, I am sure, already be waiting."

Rupert watched his mother take her leave of him, aware of the growing concern in his heart that would not fade no matter how much he tried to push it away from him. His wife was clearly upset about something and that something was, no doubt, *him*. He deserved it, of course, aware of all he had done and his many failings when it came to her, but not to know what it was particularly was quite difficult.

I could always ask her.

Shaking his head at his own thought, Rupert made his way towards the door, feeling a sense of resignation. There was nothing he could do but attend this soiree, nothing he could do but pretend that all was well for the next few hours while, inwardly, hating every moment that he stood present in society. His suffering would be all the more increased by the fact that he knew that Marie was not quite herself but at the very same time, forcing himself to be silent. He would not, *could* not bring himself to ask about her, knowing what that would do to their present standing and to his heart.

What are you going to do, then? the quiet voice of his conscience asked. *Are you going to ignore her all evening? Have her on your arm but have no interest in her?*

"Yes," Rupert said aloud, descending the stairs. "That is precisely what I intend to do." Lifting his chin, he made his way towards the drawing room, expecting some of the guests to be arriving within the next half hour. His stomach cramped at the thought of this house being filled with guests and he having nowhere to escape to.

"There you are." Martha put the back of her hand to her forehead, blowing out a long breath of seeming relief. "We were growing concerned."

"Mother came to find me," he told both Martha and Marie, who was sitting in a chair with its back to him, though she rose the moment he came around towards them. "I told her I had no intention of hiding away, if that is what you…"

He did not finish the sentence. The words began to fade from his lips as he gazed into his wife's face and felt himself swept away by her beauty.

She was astonishing.

The green of her eyes was matched by an emerald gown, with the material seeming both dark and yet shimmering with light at the very same time. Her hair was pulled to the back of her head, curls cascading down from the very top of her head to her shoulders whilst the pearls dotted within it caught the light. The rosiness in her cheeks and the soft curve of her lips beckoned to him.

Rupert groaned quietly and pushed one hand over his eyes, trying to fight the sudden swell of desire in his heart.

"You do not want to attend the soiree, we know," he heard Martha say, though to his ears, she sounded frustrated. "You do not need to show that so clearly to us both, we know it well enough already."

"It is not that," Rupert muttered, though neither Marie nor Martha pressed him on what his concern truly was. "I have said I would arrange this soiree, and I have done. Of course, I shall attend it, no matter how much I desire to stay away from everyone." Finally, he let his gaze return to his wife, though his heart leapt up all over again, making him scowl hard at his own foolishness. "Marie. Are you quite ready?"

"Wait a moment!" Martha exclaimed, coming to stand beside Marie and gesturing to her. "You are not going to say anything about how she looks? There has been much deliberation over the gown and the like and you can only stand there and ask if your wife is ready to meet the guests?" She sounded incredulous, though Rupert's embarrassment quickly grew. "I would have thought you might have said *something*, brother."

Marie waved a gentle hand in Martha's direction. "Please, there is no need to concern yourself. I am quite all right, I assure you." Turning back to Rupert, she offered him a smile but it was not the one that Rupert had been longing for. It held no light within it, no brightness nor flare of happiness. "Yes, I am quite ready. They are to greet us first before coming to the dining room or the drawing room?"

"Yes." Offering her his arm, his breath hitched when she took it, as if the heat of her hand had left a permanent scar on his arm. "The first guests will be arriving very soon."

With a nod, his wife fell into step with him and Rupert led the way through the room and out into the hallway, walking arm in arm just in case another guest should arrive to see them. They came to the front of the house and Rupert quickly released her arm, standing side by side rather than in front of each other.

The tension he felt in his frame began to tighten each and every muscle until it felt as though his very throat was being constricted. He cleared it, once, then twice before sending a sidelong glance towards his wife.

She was looking down at her hands.

Rupert closed his eyes briefly and tried to regain his composure. Here he was, ready to meet the first guests he had had at this house for some time and though he was displeased with that, he was now finding himself inexplicably concerned about Marie. Ought he to say something about her gown? About how she looked? Indeed, he had been struck by how beautiful she was but that was not something he wanted to express to *her*, not by any means! She did not need to know of his heart, not when he had made it abundantly clear to her that he did not want a single crumb of affection between them.

"You look quite resplendent, Marie." The words came out a little jerkily and to his surprise, the astonishment in her expression was so great, it took the color from her face for a moment. "*More* than suitable for a Duchess."

"I – I thank you." She stammered a little, then looked down at the floor. "I was a little anxious as to what you might think. I have never been a Duchess before."

This made his lips quirk despite himself. "You shall do excellently, I am quite sure."

When she lifted her head and looked into his eyes, the smile that came to her lips was the one that he had been longing for – whilst furious with himself for desiring it. The light in her eyes spread through her whole expression, her cheeks pinking, her smile dazzling. Her hand went back to his arm and Rupert's whole body was set alight.

"I thank you, Rupert," she said, only for the smile to fade. "I mean, Wessex. Forgive me."

"There is nothing to forgive," he said throatily, the agony in his heart of that smile shattering so quickly betraying him. "You have endured a good deal from me already, I am aware of that."

"Though I trust you now," she said, so quietly, he had to strain to hear her. "I know you will never physically injure me, for everyone I have spoken to has nothing but good to say of you."

Rupert did not know how to respond to this, a little overwhelmed to hear that there were those in his household – mother, sister and servants – who would speak good of him. Was she lying in order to bolster him a little? Or could it be that they might not see him the way he saw himself? Shaking off that last idea, he turned his gaze away but said nothing, drawing in a long breath instead.

"You do not believe me?"

"How do you do this?" Aware that his voice was a little sharp, Rupert struggled to balance it a little more. "You and my mother both seem to be aware of what it is I am thinking before I even say anything!"

A sound came from Marie that Rupert had not heard before and did not instantly recognize. Looking at her, he realized she was laughing, making his heart pound furiously, unsure as to whether she was laughing at what he had said or mocking him.

"Oh, I am not laughing at you in any condescending manner," she said, making Rupert's eyebrows lift. "Yes, I am able to see your concern, Wessex. But that is only because every emotion is written plainly on your face, it is not difficult for anyone to see precisely what it is you are thinking or feeling, for that matter. Although," she finished, her voice softening now, her head tilting to the right as she gazed up at him. "There have been times when I am sure that your outward anger has been covering over something else, something *more* that I have not been able to discern."

Rupert cleared his throat, the back of his neck prickling. He did not much like that his expressions told them everything he was thinking, though at least now he was able to understand it. "I shall have to improve my control in that regard. My expression must remain impassive."

"Oh no, pray do not!" Her hand tightened on his arm in an instant, bringing her closer to him and stealing Rupert's breath. "It is the only way I am able to know you and if you take that away from me, then I shall have nothing whatsoever."

How could he refuse her? The urge to say that no, he would do as he thought best reared up high within him but his lips refused to speak it. It was as if he was being held back by his own heart, being tugged backwards from his own desire.

It was all most disconcerting.

"And I know that you do not want to do this," she finished her hand still pressing tightly to his arm. "I understand that this is at great cost to you but that is why I value it so highly."

His lips nudged upwards into a smile but Rupert held it back, not wanting to give in. It would only bring them closer and he was doing his utmost to keep himself back from her.

"The truth is, I thought that you would turn back from this and refuse to do it," she murmured, as Rupert's lips thinned. "I had no confidence that it would actually happen, given what I know of you and what I have learned about you."

"But I did," he answered, breaking into her words.

"Yes, you did." The softness of her voice and the quiet smile on her face sent a warning into Rupert's heart. He could not have her thinking that he had done such a thing for *her* sake, even though that had, in truth, been his purpose.

"It was easier," he said, briskly, turning his head to look away from her. "For me, you understand."

There was a breath of silence. "Easier?" There was an uncertainty in her voice now, something that made Rupert's whole being tense. Did he truly wish to say this?

Surely, he told himself, firmly. *I must.*

"Easier for me, yes. It would have taken a great deal of time and effort on my part to take you to each of the gentry and visit them one at a time. That is *not* something I want to do, and though I will despise this evening and all the conversations I must have with those I do not wish to speak with, I will be able to endure it. Thus, it will all be over in a short time. You will have been introduced to everyone, I will have no further requirements to do anything else and that will be that."

The quiet which followed made Rupert feel as if his heart was shrinking within him, becoming smaller and smaller with every second that passed. All that he had just said was not the truth, he knew that full well and it sank like a heavy weight into his bones. If he was to be honest, he would have told her that he had found himself *eager* to do this for her, despite his own disinclination. He would have told her that it had been a torment to recognize that desire within him, that he had tried to find the strength to say it would not take place after all but had been unable to do so... and solely because of her. But he could not. There could not be a closeness between them. He *had* to keep her at a distance, albeit an emotional distance, for he could not let them have any sort of closeness. That would lead to affection and that, mayhap, to love and he did not deserve anything even *akin* to that. Not after all he had done.

"I see. Thank you for explaining that to me." Marie's voice was quieter now than he had ever heard it and when he glanced at her, she was looking in the opposite direction. Her hand lifted from his arm, clasped with the other and was held loosely in front of her, leaving him with a growing feeling of loss and distance.

This was what he wanted, wasn't it?

But if it was, then why did he feel increasingly miserable about getting precisely what it was he desired?

Chapter Sixteen

"It is *very* kind of you to invite us to take tea with you." Marie smiled as she picked up her tea cup, grateful that one of the new connections from the previous evening had made such an effort to reach out and build their acquaintance. "Thank you."

"Oh, but the soiree was *so* wonderful!" Miss Hamilton gushed, as her mother nodded fervently. "You know, that is the first time we have been invited to a soiree at the manor house in many a year!"

"And many feared it would never happen again!" Lady Eastgate added, though Marie quickly exchanged a look with Martha at this statement, thinking the lady a little too forward. "That must have been because the Duke was quite lonesome and none of us knew! You must be bringing him a great deal of happiness, I am sure."

Marie smiled as warmly as she could at this, praying that the two ladies would change the subject of conversation from her husband to something else. "You are both very kind."

"You know, I do think that the matter with Lord Chesterton was dealt with a somewhat poor manner," Lady Eastgate continued, waving a hand. "Though he is in France now, or so I hear. He will be back to England by the end of the month."

"And very happy!" Miss Hamilton added, as her mother reached for her tea cup. "After hearing the path that Lady Sarah took, I must say, I think that Lord Chesterton saved himself from a most unsuitable marriage. It is very good that he is so happy now."

This made Marie look at Martha again, having very little understanding as to what was being spoken of. The urge to keep the conversation away from the Duke began to fade away as she began to wonder if finding out more about Lord Chesterton's circumstances might, in some way, aid her husband. "I have not heard about Lord Chesterton's circumstances," she said, in what she hoped was a light manner. "In France, did you say?"

Lady Eastgate nodded, setting her cup down. "On his honeymoon," she said, by way of explanation. "He has been there near a year! I have heard it said he is quite besotted with Lady Prudence – though she will be Lady Chesterton now, will she not?"

"Indeed, she will," Marie murmured, glancing again to Martha, seeing her friend frowning hard. Was she upset with what Marie had asked or was this more interest and curiosity? "I do wonder if the Duke knows of Lord Chesterton's marriage, for I have not heard him mention it."

Lady Eastgate looked at her daughter. "You did think the Duke would be present, did you not?"

"I did, for I know that an invitation was sent and many expected him there," Miss Hamilton said, with a small shrug. "But he was not in attendance. Mayhap he knows of it but has not told you? I am sure, with being so recently married himself, he will have had many different things on his mind."

"Indeed, you are quite right there," Marie reassured her, not wanting to say that the Duke had not known this for fear that it would begin to spread gossip. "He must just have forgotten to tell me."

Martha set her own tea cup down. "I do not mean to gossip but I must say, I was astonished to hear of Lady Sarah! Were not you?"

Marie, who had never heard of this lady before but presumed it was the lady who had once been betrothed to Lord Chesterton, turned her attention back to the conversation.

"Disgraceful," Lady Eastgate muttered, shaking her head. "Of course, they had to marry straight away, and that even when he was already engaged! And she was courting Lord Johnstone!"

"She ought never to have drawn near Lord Whitehall, not when he was already engaged," Miss Hamilton said, with a shake of her head. "*Most* improper."

"Indeed." Martha clicked her tongue and then shook her head. "I suppose then, it is almost a blessing that Lord Chesterton was pulled from her as he did, though the manner in which that happened was not in the least bit good."

Lady Eastgate fluttered her fingers in Martha's direction. "An accident, by all accounts. Lord Chesterton himself states that he had allowed his foolishness to take a hold of him and ought never to have gone hunting in the first place."

"You have spoken with him since then?" Marie asked, unable to help herself. "You asked him about the incident?"

"Oh, yes," Miss Hamilton smiled, her eyes bright and expression warm. "I saw him at the London Season the year after, you see. Though everyone had heard about Lady Sarah by then, and he did not seem in the least bit brokenhearted. I was glad about that and then all the happier when he began to court Lady Prudence."

Martha's face split with a smile. "As was I," she said, warmly. "Now, I am afraid that our time has come to an end and we must take our leave of you."

"Though you *must* come to call at the house another time," Marie added, rising to her feet as both the other ladies smiled warmly at her. "I am so very grateful for your kindness and your friendship."

"As are we for yours, Your Grace," Lady Eastgate said, smiling at her daughter for a moment before looking back to Marie. "To have the Duchess of Wessex as one of our acquaintances is a very fine thing indeed."

Marie smiled, bobbed a curtsy and then stepped away, following after Martha. She kept her smile pinned in place as they stepped into the carriage, only to let it fall the moment the door closed and she was left alone with Martha.

"Goodness! At first, I thought their offer of friendship a wonderful thing but now I begin to fear the only reason for their desire for my company is so it lifts their own standing!"

Martha laughed and shrugged her shoulders as the carriage began the short drive home. "I am afraid that is something you will have to get used to, Marie," she said, confirming Marie's fears. "There will be many an acquaintance who wants only to take from you rather than give. Many who will be like Lady Eastgate and her daughter, especially if they have a lower title."

Marie's shoulders dropped. "That disappoints me."

"Why?"

"Because... because I wanted to have real friends," Marie answered, looking out of the window. "And I did not think it would be particularly difficult to find genuine companions."

Martha's smile became sympathetic. "You will find them, in time. Though," she continued, as Marie returned her gaze to her, "I was intrigued by what was said about Lord Chesterton! I did not know that he had wed!"

"Nor did I know about Lady Sarah," Marie added, as Martha's eyes twinkled. "But you seemed to know everything! I thought you would have said something to your brother about this before now, though mayhap you knew he would push you away before you could even open your mouth!"

A snort of laughter escaped from Martha and, as Marie looked back at her, her friend's laughter increased. When it became clear that Marie had no understanding as to what was being said, Martha quietened her laughter and spread out both hands either side.

"I did not know either."

Mouth agape, Marie stared back at her friend.

"I did not know anything," Martha continued, with a giggle. "But I did sound as though I was aware of it all, was I not?"

"Goodness me, you most certainly did!" Marie could hardly believe her ears. "Is that true? You knew nothing?"

"Nothing. However you can easily manipulate a conversation in such a way as to find out everything, especially when you have those such as Lady Eastgate and Miss Hamilton." Her smile faded, her mouth pulling flat. "They are clearly more than willing to gossip about anything and everything and I did use it to my advantage."

It took Marie a few minutes to consider all of this and though she silently did not think she would ever be able to 'manipulate a conversation' as Martha had done — and nor did she want to — she had to admit that they had learned a good deal.

"I should tell the Duke."

Martha's face fell. "Oh, my dear Marie, I know that the desire within your heart would be to tell him everything but I cannot agree that it would be wise."

"But I must!" Marie exclaimed, her heart beginning to quicken. "Can you not see, Martha? If he knows the truth about Lord Chesterton, if he hears that his friend does not hold him responsible, that he is married and on his honeymoon, *glad* that the betrothal ended, then that might lift some of the guilt from the Duke's shoulders."

Martha considered this, catching the edge of her lip between her teeth. "As much as I want to agree with you, he will not even permit you to speak of him. I know that for certain."

"I was afraid to tell him that I knew all about Lord Chesterton and the incident at the house gathering," Marie said, slowly, "but he has reassured me. I trust him now, I trust that though he might be angry with me, he will not do anything to harm me."

"So you think you will tell him? And you think he will listen?"

Considering this, Marie winced. "I cannot be sure. I think he might turn me away, might silence me before I say a single word."

Martha nodded slowly, then sighed. "But we both agree that it would be good for him to know all about Lord Chesterton and his happiness now, yes?"

"Yes."

"And he has those letters from his friend that he has not read," Martha continued, now looking out of the window and seeming to speak half to herself. "I do not know what is in them and I would very much like to find out what is said. I wish that he would read them!"

Considering this, Marie felt a nervousness come into her stomach as an idea flew into her mind. It was not at all the sort of thing she would do and certainly not something she would ever *think* to do, given that it would reflect very poorly upon her if he found out.

"You are thinking of something, are you not?"

Marie nodded slowly. "Indeed, I am. What if... what if I wrote to Lord Chesterton and asked him to come to call?"

All the color drained from Martha's face.

"I know that it would not be wise to do such a thing without asking the Duke first but you know as well as I that he would never agree to it."

"No, he would not."

"But it is the only way for this to be resolved," Marie said, quietly. "I am afraid that he will hate me for doing such a thing, but it is a risk I must take." Her heart quailed within her and she looked down at her hands. "I confess that there have been times of late where I have found myself lost in a dream. A dream of what my life might be like if the Duke was as you once described him to be, Martha."

Martha's lips curved lightly. "My mother has been concerned for you, given that you have been so often 'lost in a dream', as you have said."

"You have noticed?"

Her friend nodded. "I reassured her and said all was well... but you have been thinking about Wessex?"

"I have," Marie admitted, feeling no shame in confessing the truth. "The soiree went better than I expected, though he did not smile once."

"But he did speak with everyone and introduced you to each and every person, which I was glad to see," Martha added, as Marie smiled to herself, thinking on how well the evening had gone. The Duke had not altered himself in any way, of course, had not had very much to say, had not shown any sort of enjoyment or even happiness but he *had* done his duty in remaining with her for the majority of the evening and making sure she was acquainted with everyone. Whether any of the other guests had noticed his dark demeanor, Marie could not say even if she felt quite certain they had. Mayhap, that was all they expected now.

"I do think there was something in that," Martha said, pulling Marie from her thoughts. "In throwing that soiree for you."

"Oh, but he did not throw it for me," Marie countered quickly, feeling the same stab of pain in her heart that had come when the Duke himself had told her as much. There had been a twinge of happiness in her heart before that moment, finding their connection strengthening *just* a little, but he had taken that all from her before she had even had a chance to enjoy it.

"Whatever do you mean?"

Marie shrugged and tried to look as though it did not mean much to her. "He stated that it was because it was easier for *him* to do it this way. It meant he did not have to take me to each and every house, did not have to drink tea with them all individually and the like." She tried to smile but there was something in her voice which she could not hide. "It was primarily for his benefit, you understand."

The shout of laughter at this made Marie jump in surprise. "He told you that?"

"Yes, he did."

"And you believed him?" Martha asked, with a wide-eyed look. "My dear friend, if he had wanted to take the burden from himself, he would have had my mother or myself make the introductions to the gentry. Indeed, I think Mother had already offered or suggested that she would do such a thing, did she not?"

Marie blinked rapidly, the pain in her heart quickly lessening. "I had not thought of that." Her brows furrowed. "Why would he say such a thing?"

Martha tilted her head. "Might it be that he did not want you to have any sort of hope of a connection between you? That he wanted to hide his true desire from you?"

Closing her eyes, Marie took this in, feeling herself torn between relief and confusion. "Mayhap he saw the hope in me." Her eyes opened. "I do not know what it is that I am hoping for but there is hope there nonetheless... and I must do something with it."

Martha smiled, hesitated and then looked away. "Mother and I have been near to desperation in our attempts to have him relieve himself from this burden he carries. In truth, I think both she and I have almost given up, given that he is so very determined to cling to this guilt."

The idea that Marie had of speaking to Lord Chesterton now settled itself very firmly in her mind. It seemed to be the only way forward, the only thing she could think to do that might bring about any sort of change. "Then I must do this," she said, quietly. "I *must* find a way to have Lord Chesterton come here, so that he can speak to Wessex directly and explain his present circumstances."

"And that he does not hold anything against him," Martha put in, as Marie nodded. "You are right, I think. The only way my brother will listen is if the words come directly from Lord Chesterton. Though..." Trailing off, she bit her lip and looked down at her hands. "There is a very high chance that my brother will near to disavow you should he be angry about what you have done. It could all go very badly indeed."

Accepting this, Marie's heart began to hammer furiously, aware of what it was she had so desperately begun to hope for and how even considering this might put the connection between them entirely awry. If it was true what Martha had said, if it was true that the Duke had been trying to make certain she had no hope whatsoever of a connection between them, then the little that she had felt growing between them would be ruined completely if he set himself against her.

And yet, she thought, *there is no hope of it growing if I do nothing. He is clearly determined to set us apart, no matter what it is he might be feeling.* Her heart lurched as she recalled the way she had looked into his eyes and seen the pain burning there. Had she not felt as though he wanted to lean in close to her? How he wanted to pull her near but his own guilt would not let him do such a thing?

"I must risk all," she said, as Martha gazed back at her, steadily. "I have no choice. I cannot let our future be as dark and as dull as it is at present. Once you return to your husband and your mother goes to the Dower house, I shall be almost entirely alone and I do not think that will do me any good."

"Especially if you have a growing, steady hope for all that might be," Martha said, gently, as heat began to grow in Marie's cheeks. "I can only agree. It is a great risk, indeed, but if you are determined, if you are set, then I shall do all that I can to help you."

Relief poured into Marie's heart. "I thank you, Martha."

"Then what must we do?"

Thinking quickly, Marie's shoulders lifted. "I think we must find how to write to Lord Chesterton. Whether we get the return address from the Duke's letters or from some other means, we must find it."

"I know exactly who we can ask," came the urgent reply. "And, if fate smiles on us, we shall be able to write a letter this very day."

"The Duke must not know of it," Marie said, fear beginning to crawl up her spine, worried that her plan would come to a crashing halt before it had even begun. "He cannot know of the letter."

"He will not," Martha assured her. "I know which of the servants we can trust. Wessex will be kept quite in the dark."

"Until," Marie murmured to herself, "until it is much too late for him to do anything other than step into the light."

Chapter Seventeen

Rupert threw back his head and yawned. Stretching wide, he pushed himself back up into his chair and then shook his head to clear his vision.

I should retire.

He had been awake for far too long, looking into his business affairs carefully, so that he might assess whether or not he was making the wisest decisions when it came to his investments. His man of business in London was very particular, making sure that everything was sent to Rupert promptly and with the finest detail. Thus far, Rupert was contented, though he did have questions over his most present investment – a ship. It had taken its maiden voyage but had not, as yet, returned confirmation of its safe arrival. That left Rupert feeling a little unsure.

"But enough," he muttered to himself, rubbing one hand over his face. "I must retire."

Still, there was reluctance there. Rupert knew full well that the only reason for his reluctance was because, when he finally entered his bed, his dreams would be full of Marie. If she did not haunt his thoughts, then she would stumble into his dreams and remain there. Though at least, in his dreams, he was able to take her into his arms, to apologise profusely for his ill manner and his coldness towards her and beg her for forgiveness, before pressing his lips to hers. In that dream, at least, he was truly happy, but every time he awoke, the heaviness returned in an instant. He could never do such a thing, of course. One day soon, he would have to take her to bed but it would have to be an emotionless affair. To let his heart free to care for her would be foolish, for he could not trust himself with such a precious creature. After all he had done to Lord Chesterton, Rupert was too afraid to permit himself to grow close to her, even if that was what his heart so desperately wanted.

"Perhaps I shall not think of her tonight," he muttered to himself, making his way out of the study and towards his own rooms. "Mayhap I shall be too exhausted to do anything but sleep."

As he walked down the hallway, a small chink of light emanating from an open door caught his attention. It was late enough that every servant had retired, for Rupert had dismissed them all soon after dinner had been served. Martha, Marie and his mother had all retired, so why was the door to the library open? Frowning, Rupert walked towards it and quietly pushed open the door, not wanting to disturb his mother if it was she within.

It was not.

His breath hitched as he took in his wife. She was asleep in a chair, her hair undone and cascading gently down her shoulders to her waist. Clad in her night gown, her head was pressed to the side of the chair, her eyes closed and a book fallen in her lap, though her fingers were still within the pages. Mayhap she had been unable to sleep and had come to the library to find something to read, only to find herself overcome. The delicate beauty of her made his heart ache, seeing the soft pink in her cheeks, the steady rise and fall of her breath.

I cannot.

Rupert caught himself as he made to step closer to her, realizing too late what the urge in his heart compelled him to do. He wanted to go to her, to catch her up in his arms and hold her close, ready to lift her to her bedchamber as any husband might.

A husband who cared for his wife, at least.

And I do, he confessed silently, still unable to drag his gaze away from her. *I do care for her despite my efforts to push her away. I know so little about her and the urge within me is to know her all the better,* not *to push her away. Why must I be so foolish? Why must I have such ridiculous desires?*

As if his thoughts had been spoken aloud, Marie stirred but her eyes did not open. Rupert hesitated, his whole body tingling now with the desire to step closer to her though his heart and mind warred against each other.

"Rupert."

He started, then, his heart beating furiously as embarrassment burned up into his face. She was awake, then? She had seen him standing there, wondering perhaps why he simply gazed at her in silence?

"Marie, I –"

His feet moved of their own accord, taking him soundlessly across the carpet towards her but the words on his lips faded quickly away. Gazing down at her, he realized she *was* asleep, that his name had been uttered whilst in a dream. That thought made his stomach flip, his eyes widening as he wondered what exactly it was she was dreaming of.

A fervent hope began to burn and Rupert could not seem to extinguish it. Groaning aloud, he tried his utmost to keep himself back from her, to stop himself from doing what his heart was near forcing him to do… only for the fight to fade and one determination to linger.

"Marie?" Bending low, he whispered her name but she did not move. Rupert hesitated, struggling to know quite how he ought to lift her up into his arms. Slipping one arm behind her head and around to her shoulder, he somehow managed to lift her gently, though the book fell to the floor with a thump as he straightened.

"Oh!" Marie's eyes flew open and she looked up at him, her face inches from his. Rupert did not know what to say, his mouth going dry, his heart thundering wildly, wondering if he ought to now set her back to her feet, excuse himself and then walk from the room.

"Oh." This time, there was no surprise in that word. Instead, there was only a softness, almost a contentedness that made the corners of her lips curve upwards. Her eyes fluttered closed and, much to Rupert's surprise, her head rested gently against his shoulder as though she was glad he was there, glad that he held her so closely.

A knot tied itself in his throat as he began to carry her from the library out into the hallway. There was something in this that he had never felt before but he dared not give it too great a thought for fear that it would take a hold of him and never let him go. Even this, what he was doing by holding her as he was, spoke of sheer foolishness on his part! It *was* bringing them closer in a way he had tried to reject for the last few weeks! Nonetheless, he had not been able to prevent himself from taking her in his arms.

Laying her down gently in her bed, Rupert could not help himself from brushing a long strand of hair from her cheek, setting it on the pillow instead. It felt like silk in his fingers, making his heart thunder.

"Rupert," she said, softly, reaching up to find his hand, though her eyes still stayed closed. Licking his lips and telling himself he ought to already have left her and gone to his own rooms, Rupert waited where he was, her hand in his as she slowly drifted off to sleep again. While her fingers went limp and still, Rupert stood there, holding her hand and gazing down at her as though she was the most magnificently beautiful woman he had ever seen.

Quite how long he stood there for, he could not say. It was with great reluctance, however, reluctance that screamed at him to stop when he tried to leave, that he finally set her hand down and stepped back.

I fear I am falling in love with her, he told himself, miserably. *And that is a dreadful thing indeed.*

Chapter Eighteen

Two weeks later.

"Marie?"

She looked up, her lips lifting into a smile as the Duke came into the room. "Rupert, good afternoon."

"Good afternoon." He did not come to sit beside her but set both hands to a chair, looking back at her. There had been a change in their relationship this last fortnight, though Marie could not quite state what it was. Ever since he had lifted her into his arms and carried her to her bed, he had seemed to *want* to be with her, had come to seek her out on many more occasions than he had done previously.

But all the same, he had held himself back. There had been a wariness there, a hesitancy that she had not been able to break through. Despite having enjoyed a good many conversations and despite having begun to sit with them all at dinner and appearing almost jovial at times, he still would not come close to her.

And it was the one thing that Marie was slowly beginning to desire above all other.

"I have come to ask you about the dinner menu for next week," he said, frowning. "If you recall, my mother has invited Lord and Lady Granger to dine with us."

"Yes, I remember."

"She is also intending to remove to the Dower house very soon," he said, changing the topic of conversation so quickly, Marie's breath caught. "Once Martha has taken her leave at the end of next week, she too will then remove from the house."

Marie's whole body tightened as a wave of confusion washed over her. She had very much enjoyed the Dowager's company and Martha's also, but she had also known it would not last forever. The Dowager had her own house to reside in and Martha would soon return to her husband.

Which meant that she would be left alone with the Duke for the first time since they had wed.

"You are upset by that, I see."

Looking back at her husband, Marie took a moment before she replied, considering all that she felt. "I will miss them both."

"You are not the only one whose emotions are sometimes displayed on one's face," he said, with what appeared to be a hint of a smile. Thus far, she had never seen him smile, leaving her wondering whether or not it would transform his expression entirely. "I am sorry to see you sad."

"The Dower House is not far away, is it?"

He shook his head, emerging from behind the chair—one which Marie believed he had employed as a barricade—and then took his place beside her, though he maintained as much space as possible between them, seating himself near the very edge of his seat. "It is not too far away at all. I have every expectation that my mother will still come to dine with us at least three times a week. More, if you will have her."

"I would be very glad to see her as often as she likes," Marie answered, looking into the Duke's blue eyes and thinking to herself that they were a little lighter today. Whenever he had been in a temper, she had seen them dark and stormy but today, there was nothing but calmness there. "And if I am to be truthful, Rupert, I do confess to being a trifle concerned about being alone in the house. I have been used to company and though I am still very much a bluestocking, books do not give the same comfort as good company."

"But you shall not be alone."

Whether he had meant to do so or not, the Duke reached out and took Marie's hand, pressing it lightly but as Marie looked down in surprise, he quickly withdrew it.

"I shall be here, of course," he said, now clasping his hands tightly in his lap as if he feared that, if he did not, he would take her hand again. "I am not so very dull and dark these days, am I?"

This made her smile. "You are certainly less so," she admitted, gently, not wanting to injure him with her words. "I have enjoyed our conversations and I know that your mother and your sister have been very glad to see you in better mood.

This made the Duke smile, though it was a rueful one. A thrill ran up Marie's spine, seeing how his eyes glinted and how his whole face lightened. This was a hint of the gentleman she wanted so very much to know. Slowly but surely, she prayed, he was returning to himself.

And Lord Chesterton must have received my letter by now, she thought to herself, a nervousness fluttering in her stomach. *I must hope to receive his reply soon.*

"I suppose my mood has been a little improved, though it may improve all the more once Martha returns to her husband." His lips quirked again. "I do care for my sister a great deal but she has always been talkative."

Marie laughed at this, boldly reaching out to take his hand. "I agree, of course, but I find that an excellent and endearing quality, I confess. I very much appreciate that about her, for I have always liked talking and discussing things."

The Duke tipped his head just a little, his eyes assessing. "You and I have spent a little more time in conversation these last few weeks, have we not?"

Her heart quickened as she nodded, wondering what it was he meant by such a remark.

"That has been... unexpected."

"I quite agree," Marie said, softly. "You have not been dismayed by that, I hope?"

He shook his head but said nothing, a slight frown beginning to pull at his forehead.

"I have found it quite delightful," she admitted, deciding to be honest with him. "I am worried, though, that once your mother and sister take their leave, you will also do the same."

"Leave?" That frown grew heavier. "This is my home, Marie. Why would I leave?"

"I do not mean in that sense," Marie told him, her fingers pressing to his a little more, quite surprised that he had not withdrawn them as yet. "More that you will return to how you were when we were first wed. That you will retreat, draw back from me and will leave me all alone. Indeed," she continued, quickly as he opened his mouth, "I am well aware that we had stipulations and that we signed them together, but that does seem to have changed a little, has it not?"

A long, steady breath escaped from his mouth as he gazed into her eyes, seemingly unwilling to answer. A touch of heat rose in Marie's cheeks and she looked away from him, mortified that she had spoken so honestly and yet without any seeming understanding from him. "Mayhap it is just I who sees it that way, but I have been glad of it, at least."

"No, it is not just you who has seen it." What sounded like a pained sigh came from him, forcing Marie's eyes back towards him. "I did not want to do this."

"Oh." Her heart sank, her shoulders rounding. "I thought —"

"It has been impossible for me to do anything other than this, however," he interrupted her, a slight pressure being returned to her fingers though he did not move even a fraction closer to her. "I have regretted it every single day, sitting in my bedchamber and realising what a fool I have been."

Confused, Marie frowned and shifted closer to him, but he instantly leaned back. "What is it that makes you a fool?" she asked, aware that she felt a trifle insulted even if she did not believe that he had meant to do such a thing. "Why does spending time with your wife make you a fool?"

"It... it is because I have clung to solitude for so long, because it is all that I deserve." The edge of his voice cracked just a little though his gaze remained steady. "I cannot permit myself to be anything more than briefly acquainted with you, but it seems that intention has failed entirely, has it not?" Again, his lips lifted but it was sadness which filled his gaze now. "You said that you knew all that had taken place, so you must understand."

"No, I do not!" she exclaimed, moving even closer to him now, her other hand going to settle on their joined ones. "I think you wrong to burden yourself as you have done."

He shook his head and looked away from her, though he did not pull his hand back. "Then you are mistaken. You have been listening to my mother and to Martha and they have influenced you. They want so very much for my guilt to be gone from me, they cannot see the truth."

"Or mayhap it is *you* who cannot see it," she answered, leaning towards him as desperation flooded her. Ought she to tell him what she knew of Lord Chesterton? Was now the moment to do so? Mayhap she did not need him to come to call after all, not if the Duke would be willing to listen to her now. "Could it not be that you have burdened yourself with a weight that no one but you thinks you ought to be carrying? What if *you* are wrong and we are all correct in our judgements?"

The Duke scowled and lifted his hand, retreating from her. "You cannot know. You were not present."

"I – I know I was not but all the same, I think you have burdened yourself unnecessarily." Beginning to panic, seeing how he pulled away from her, Marie grasped his hand tightly again, leaning towards him. "Can you not see what might now be, if only you would set the past aside?"

The way he let out a hiss of breath, the way his eyes flared and his hand squeezed hers told her exactly what she wanted to know. He *did* see it, *did* want it and yet could not bring himself to step free of the past. Her heart ached, both with longing and with doubt, worrying about what would happen if she dared act.

"Marie," he said, his voice rasping, "I cannot. I fear I would only bring you harm one day, in the way I brought harm to Lord Chesterton. I do not trust myself."

She took in a breath, lifted her chin and looked straight into his eyes. "But I trust you."

Marie had never kissed anyone before. She did not know what she was doing, did not know what she was *meant* to do, but the desire to be held close in his arms was enough to push her into action. Leaning into him, she put one hand around his neck and pressed her lips to his.

She felt him start, his whole body tensing as her fingers brushed the nape of his neck. Every part of her was aflame, burning with a heat that had never before come into her body. Her hand was clutching his now, almost desperate for him to respond... and, after a few moments, he did.

His free hand went to her arm, then ran up lightly to her shoulder and then to her neck, his head slanting just a little so the kiss deepened. Marie felt as though she were spiraling, twisting this way and that as light and color exploded in her head.

"No!"

One moment, she was lost in his embrace, the next, she was left cold, gasping for air when the Duke almost threw her back as he rose to his feet, backing away from her.

"I cannot!" he exclaimed, a wild look in his eyes, one hand and then the next pushing through his hair. "Why must you do this to me?"

Marie, still breathing hard, reached out one hand to him. "Rupert, there is nothing wrong. You are my *husband*, are you not?"

His eyes closed. "That may be so but I cannot let my heart free. I do not deserve it, Marie. I never shall."

Without another word, he spun around and hurried out of the room, leaving Marie staring at nothing but a closed door.

Her heart was pounding furiously, her eyes suddenly damp with tears as she realized he had left her alone and had no intention of returning. She had taken a risk and it had ended dreadfully, leaving her with even more of a taste of what happiness and joy might be in her future while, at the same time, leaving her with nothing but sorrow.

Pulling out her handkerchief, Marie pressed it to her eyes, feeling herself shaking. That had been one of the most wonderful experiences of her life and now, in the moments that had followed and the shock that had come with his hasty departure, she was left feeling empty and completely broken.

"Marie, are you in here?"

Marie had only a moment to stuff her handkerchief away before the door opened and Martha stepped inside, though her smile quickly faded when she took in Marie's expression. "What has happened?"

Marie did her best to smile and to dismiss her friend's concerns, but it did not work. Tears came instead of her smile, her heart crying out in pain and dampness, once more.

"What is it?" Martha wrapped one arm around her shoulders, her eyes wide with worry. "Has something happened? Was my brother truly awful to you?"

"No, he was not," Marie answered, hoarsely, as Martha's comfort soothed her heart just a little. "He was wonderful, though only for a moment."

This seemed to bring some sort of understanding, for Martha immediately let out a slow sigh, shaking her head lightly. "Oh, my dear friend. I did think that such a thing might happen."

"You did?" Marie, wiping her eyes, turned her head to look at her. "What do you mean?"

"I have seen my brother change, as have you," Martha told her, gently. "It is because of you, Marie. This is all because of you." Her smile grew a little. "He is quite in love with you and he does not know what to do with that."

This did not bring Marie any happiness nor relief. "He does not want to feel that way, I know that. He made it abundantly clear that he cannot have any sort of affection for me, that he does not *want* to have any closeness with me."

"Is that what he said?"

Marie closed her eyes to prevent yet more tears from falling. "It is not only what he said but what he evidenced by walking away from me."

"I am sorry for that." Another sigh came as Martha shook her head. "I do not know what to do."

Holding back her tears with an effort, Marie crumpled her handkerchief in her hand. "Lord Chesterton is my only hope at this juncture, I think."

"You are to go ahead with your plan, then?"

She nodded, a fresh determination beginning to grow within her. After all that she had just shared with the Duke, after the hint of what might be had been given to her to taste, she was not about to let it all go now. Indeed, taking this risk and kissing him had ended badly but that did not mean she was going to hold herself back from this for fear that it might happen again. "It is the only thing I can do," she said, quietly. "And I am determined to do it."

Chapter Nineteen

Rupert ran one hand over his eyes, feeling them hot and gritty. It had been five days since he had seen another living soul, aside from his butler and one of the maids. Five days since he had closed himself away, five days since he had shared a kiss with his wife and five days of utter torment.

A groan broke from his lips as he threw himself back in his chair, trying and failing to concentrate on the matters at hand. His business affairs had been sitting in the same pile as they had been for the last sennight, having been quite unable to concentrate on anything but her.

This was the most dreadful circumstance he had ever found himself in. He tried to pretend he did not want to have anything to do with his wife, had told himself repeatedly of how little he needed her, yet he knew all too well that he spoke nothing but lies to himself. All of his plans to keep himself far from her had broken apart into nothing more than dust and ashes. Now, his desire was to be with her, to be in her company as much as he could, to see her smile and to smile at *him*. He wanted to see the light in her eyes, to see the pink in her cheeks and the curve of her lips – and he wanted then to take her in his arms and kiss her with all the passion and affection he felt.

But I cannot. Closing his eyes, a vision of Lord Chesterton rose in his mind, recalling the moment he had ridden into the clearing and seen his friend so grievously injured. He had been the cause of that, for his own decision had caused Lord Chesterton's injury. The pain and suffering Lord Chesterton had endured had been all because of him also and now, Rupert could not bring himself to ever allow himself close to another. What if another foolish word left his lips? What if a decision he made caused such pain to another? He could not bring himself to even *think* on that, shuddering violently as he thought of Marie. If she was ever brought to pain and suffering because of him, he would never be able to forgive himself.

And yet, I think I am in love with her.

That was what made it such a dreadful circumstance. He was slowly being torn apart, for he could not have love in his heart while at the very same time, try to pluck it out of himself and throw it away. It was a battle Rupert already knew he would not win, for to go on with his wife in this house for years to come meant that there would be no respite. His foolish heart would only increase in its affection for her, he was sure, and he did not know what to about that.

"Wessex?"

"No, Mother." Rupert held up one hand, palm out as the door opened. "I do not want company."

"You shall have it nonetheless," she said, coming into the room and standing in front of him. "I have given you near enough a sennight to be alone and now I have come to speak with you." Her eyebrow arched. "You are aware that Martha and I have both delayed our plans to depart, are you not?"

Groaning aloud, Rupert dropped his head into his hands. "Why must you torment me?"

"Oh, it is not for *your* sake that we linger," she said, briskly, "but for your wife. What do you think your absence has done to *her*? Or is it that you are so wrapped up in your own thoughts and feelings, you have quite forgotten about hers?"

Guilt sent Rupert's stomach dipping low. "I have not forgotten."

"Then why, when you were only just beginning to improve, when we were all so happy to see you happier, have you retreated?" She came another step closer though the desk was still between them. "You cannot hide away from her forever, Rupert."

The softness in his mother's voice, the gentle way she smiled at him and the glint in her eye told Rupert that she knew exactly what it was he was feeling.

"You know I do not deserve any happiness," he said, throatily, feeling as though he had nothing left to give, no strength to even keep his thoughts to himself. "I cannot trust myself when I am near her and thus, I must step back."

"But she is your *wife*," his mother said, emphatically. "You are going to have to be close to her! That is how one lives when one is wed. One's life is shared and that is a beautiful thing, in many ways."

"I deserve no beauty."

The Dowager's face crumpled. "*You* are the only one who thinks so."

Rupert shook his head. "I am quite sure I am not."

At this, his mother thumped one hand on his study desk, astonishing Rupert with such an action. "Then I shall prove it to you," she said, firmly. "You are to come to the drawing room in half an hour, Wessex. I will not have you disagree."

"The drawing room?" Rupert shook his head. "No, Mother. You know that I have been seeking out my solitude of late."

"I care nothing for that. You do it to punish yourself, as though you *deserve* it," she answered, a hint of frustration in her voice now. "You shall come to the drawing room, Wessex, or I shall bring us all to you."

With that, she turned and hurried to the door as if she did not want to give him opportunity to say anything more. Rupert was about to protest, to say that he would lock the door to his study to prevent her from returning, only to realize that his mother would, no doubt, simply bang repeatedly on the door until he would not be able to take it any longer and would open to her. His own frustration beginning to burn, he shoved one hand through his hair, threw his head back and squeezed his eyes closed.

I have no choice, he told himself, angry now. *But I have time. Time to prepare myself* and *my heart so when I see Marie, I will not be affected.*

His head lowered, his heart beginning to quicken even at the thought of setting his gaze upon Marie again. No matter how long he prepared, no matter how much time he gave himself, Rupert was quite sure he would find himself in difficulty the second his eyes met hers.

***

Closing his eyes, Rupert paused just outside the drawing room door. He did not want to be here. The only place he wanted to be was back in his study, with the door locked and bolted.

But he had no choice.

His heart was doing quite the opposite of his mind, leaping about in joyful anticipation as his mind ran through all the worrisome feelings that would soon affect him. Feeling as if he were coming apart, he took in a deep breath, gripped the handle and, with another breath, stepped inside.

A flurry of movement met him.

"You are here, thank goodness." His mother practically ran at him as both Martha and Marie rose to their feet, standing together side by side. "Come in." Instead of leading him, she came behind him and closed the door as a footman might, making Rupert frown, glancing behind him in confusion.

"Thank you for coming, Rupert." It was Marie who spoke this time but Rupert averted his gaze, despite the screaming in his heart to let his eyes meld with hers. "I know this will be difficult but you must know we have only the best for you in our thoughts."

"What will be difficult?" Rupert said, frowning. "I do not —"

A movement in the corner of the room caught his attention. He turned his head to look, only to reel backwards, stumbling and almost falling to the floor. Hitting the wall, he spread out his arms flat against it, breathing hard, eyes staring.

"Wessex." The gentleman came closer to him, one hand to his heart. "You cannot know the joy in my heart at seeing you."

Rupert closed his eyes tightly, then opened them again, half praying he was seeing an apparition. It could not be. It could not *be*!

What was Lord Chesterton doing here?

"You do not want to see me, I know. Nor do you want to read my letters," Lord Chesterton said, taking another step or two towards him. "I wish that you would have done so, my friend."

"Friend?" Rupert rasped, his throat burning, chest painfully tight as he fought to drag in air. "Why are you here?"

Lord Chesterton smiled lightly. "I am here because your wife cares so much for you — as does your mother and your sister."

Rupert dragged his gaze away from Lord Chesterton towards Marie, who was now standing, white faced, with one hand at her mouth. Martha had an arm around her waist for support, though she too was watching them both with wide eyes. "*You* did this?" The question was pointed at his wife but Martha and his mother were quick to respond.

"We both agreed it was the best course of action," Martha said quickly, as Marie gave him a small, sharp nod while tears flooded in her eyes all the same.

"Yes, we did. And I am glad we did so, for to see the way you have retreated all the more has brought us all a great weight of concern." His mother tilted her chin upwards, though she remained close to the door as if she was concerned he might flee from them all. "We knew you would not listen to us speaking about the situation, so we had no other choice but this."

Rupert closed his eyes again, feeling as though he were drowning with no way to gasp for air.

"You must listen to me, my friend," Lord Chesterton said, firmly. "I have tried to write to you to explain and you would not read my letters, it seemed. I heard that you had become a recluse and though it was on my mind to come to call, I felt certain you would not see me."

Opening his eyes, Rupert looked down at the floor as he tried to stand tall, weakness beginning to steal away every bit of strength from him. "Chesterton, please. You need not say a word. I already know my guilt; I have no need for you to explain it to me."

"Guilt?"

The surprise in Lord Chesterton's voice made Rupert's head lift, wondering why he sounded so astonished.

"There is no guilt on your part, Wessex," Lord Chesterton said slowly, every word given great weight and meaning. "I hold nothing against you. Not a single thing."

Rupert blinked furiously, not able to comprehend what was being said.

"Shall we sit down?" his friend asked, coming to stand close to Rupert now, putting one hand on his shoulder. "There is much I need to say to you. All I ask you to do is listen."

A slight dizziness told a hold of his head as Rupert tried to nod, numbness spreading through him. With weighted steps, he somehow found his way to a chair, sitting down heavily in it. A glass of brandy was pressed into his hands by his wife but Rupert did not look up at her. She was the cause of this. She was the reason that the one person he had not been able to think of without pain was now sitting opposite him.

It was all her doing, all her fault and Rupert could not bring himself to look into her eyes any more.

Chapter Twenty

Marie held back her tears as she sat down, relieved when Martha rang the bell for the tea tray to be brought in, quite sure she needed the sustenance it would bring. She had seen how the Duke would not look at her, had seen the shock still ravaging his expression and knew he held her responsible for this.

The scratch at the door told her the maid was present, though the Dowager rose to her feet and went to bring it from the very door itself rather than let the maid in. They had all discussed the concern that the Duke might flee from them if he had the chance and, even though he was now seated, it was clear that the Dowager still held such concern.

When Lord Chesterton had arrived earlier that day, it had been nothing but difficult to keep his presence hidden from the Duke. The Dowager had informed the butler and the staff, in no uncertain terms, that his presence was to be kept from the Duke until she arranged for them to meet and, even though she was not the authority in the house, they had clearly all agreed to do so. Marie had though to herself that even the servants must have known the reason for the Duke's quiet manner and, therefore, were willing to do as was asked in the hope that he might return to the master of the house he had once been.

What had followed thereafter had been a long and lengthy conversation with Lord Chesterton, where she had explained not only her reason for writing to him but also the secrecy with which he was, at present, concealed in the house. Martha had told Lord Chesterton about her brother's sorrow and guilt, had explained about his retreat from all and sundry and Marie herself had seen the sadness in Lord Chesterton's eyes. He had explained his own situation and had seemed eager to explain all to the Duke himself.

Now all that mattered was whether or not the Duke would listen.

Chewing on the edge of her lip, she barely noticed the tea cup set in front of her. The Duke had not said a word as yet, though he had almost drained the brandy glass already. Lord Chesterton was sitting quietly also, his own glass of brandy sitting on the table in front of him rather than being held in his hand. He was looking at Rupert steadily, though the Duke himself appeared to be doing all he could to avert his gaze.

Please let this conversation change all. Her breathing quickened as Rupert finally looked at her but he pulled his gaze away from her as quickly as he could.

"Thank you, Martha." The Dowager smiled at her daughter and then looked to her son. "Rupert, I hope you will listen."

"It seems as though I have no choice," he muttered, one hand passing over his eyes. "I did not know I was to be ambushed." His hand dropped down to his lap again and he sent a sharp, narrowed dart of a glance towards Marie. "I cannot believe that you would think to attack me in such a way."

"It is not an attack!" she protested at once, hot tears in her eyes. "My only reason for this is to *help* you... to help us all." This did not seem to bring the Duke any relief nor did he show any understanding. Instead, he turned his head away directly and looked down at his brandy glass as though it would give him more comfort than she could.

"I know that you took things very badly – and personally," Lord Chesterton said, speaking directly to the Duke. "But you need not do so. I wish that you had *not* done so, for it would have saved you years of unhappiness and prevented such pain."

The Duke shook his head but did not lift his gaze. "I was the one responsible for your injury," he said, his voice quiet but his shoulders rounding with heaviness. "I did not force you from that horse, I did not insist strongly enough."

"Because you are a good, considerate friend who knew that I would do what I wished regardless," Lord Chesterton responded, quickly. "I was far too much in my cups to go riding, indeed, but I managed it all the same. And you, given that you had other guests at the house gathering, were, I am sure, a little uncertain about the scene I might cause were you to refuse me with any sort of strength."

Marie reached for her tea, hearing it rattle lightly as she lifted it, yet she could not take her eyes nor her attention from her husband. Was this going to have any effect upon him? Would he change his mind about his own guilt?

"I could have and should have done more."

"No." Lord Chesterton's voice was firm. "You have no guilt here. *I* snatched the prepared gun from your man, *I* let my own stubbornness and pride take a hold of me. I was the one who caused my injury, not you."

"I – I still do not know how it happened." Rupert did not respond to anything Lord Chesterton had said directly but spoke of the accident itself. "The gun, how did it –"

"It was not your fault," Lord Chesterton said, again. "I was foolish and heavy handed. In my drunken state, I was not careful in how I held the gun and in trying to hold it, it slipped from my hand. That is how I sustained an injury to my leg. Though," he finished, "in many ways, I am grateful for what happened."

This made Marie's heart slam hard against her chest as the Duke's head lifted sharply, his eyes going straight to Lord Chesterton. Silence filled the room as he stared, in clear astonishment, at Lord Chesterton though he did not say a word. Lord Chesterton held the Duke's gaze steadily and Marie, reaching out, gripped Martha's hand. Was he going to listen to Lord Chesterton's explanation? And if he did, would it make any difference to him?

"Should you like me to explain?" Lord Chesterton asked, speaking so quietly as if he did not want to break the silence. "I will be happy to tell you all, my friend."

"I cannot believe you would even say such a thing as that," the Duke said, not answering Lord Chesterton's question. "Are you trying to appease me in some way? Trying to take this burden from me for the sake of my family?"

"Listen to him, please!" Marie, unable to keep silent, leaned forward in her chair though her husband did not look at her. "Your mother, your sister and I have all tried to tell you the same thing as this so many times and you refused to even speak of it. Now, Lord Chesterton is here to tell you the truth and, without even waiting for his explanation, you are choosing not to believe him and his motivations? Why can you not simply trust that he is telling you the truth? That he does not see things the way you do?"

Again, a silence fell but it did not last as long as the previous quiet. After a few moments, the Duke let out a slow breath and then gestured to Lord Chesterton. "The truth is, Chesterton, it is because of my mother and my sister's determined attempts to remove this guilt from me that I cannot trust your words. You, being as good and as generous as you are, will look upon this situation and do whatever you can to help. That does not mean that you do not think me responsible for your injury and for all that came after it. It only means that your heart is far more kind and far more generous than it ought to be."

"Or," Lord Chesterton responded, quickly, "it means that *your* heart is much too accusatory and distrustful."

Marie snatched in a breath. Lord Chesterton was speaking far more bluntly than she had ever been and thus far, it appeared to be making some sort of impact given the way the Duke frowned, ran a hand over his chin and then slowly began to nod. Hope began to burn a little more brightly now as Lord Chesterton reached for his brandy glass, took a sip and then began.

"When I say that I am grateful, it is because I am," he said, his voice a little louder now, more confident and stronger. "You might be more than astonished to hear me say such a thing and indeed, you might disbelieve me, as I see you do. But it is the truth."

"How can that be?" the Duke asked, a crack in his voice. "You lost so much, that day. Your leg... I was told there would always be a weakness there. And then Lady Sarah and the betrothal... I know how much you cared for her, Chesterton. And I was the one who tore her away from you."

"I will not accept that from you." Lord Chesterton sat forward in his chair. "Lady Sarah made her own decisions, did she not?"

"But if you had not been so injured, then she would never have stepped away from you!"

"And what good would that have been to me?"

Marie could see the way the Duke's confusion began to take over his expression. His eyes darted away from Lord Chesterton and then returned again, lines drawn between his brows as he ran one finger lightly over his lips. She knew what Lord Chesterton wanted to say and was almost fervent in her desire for him to explain. It might be the one thing that would bring the Duke some relief.

"Do you not understand?" Lord Chesterton asked, with such a gentleness in his voice that Marie wanted to weep. "My friend, it showed me the truth of her character. She was shallow in her affections and, in truth, a deceiver."

Marie's stomach dipped. "She did not tell you the truth, you mean?"

Both gentlemen looked to her at once, and for the first time, the Duke's eyes met hers, making her shiver. There were shadows lingering there, though they were, she hoped, beginning to fade.

"That is, it precisely, Your Grace," Lord Chesterton answered, with a small, sad smile. "She told me how much her heart yearned for me, declared herself quite in love with me and then, when it was discovered that I might have a weakness in my leg, she deserted me."

"Only to then prove her character less than pleasing in an even worse manner!" The Duchess tossed her head, then clicked her tongue. "I am glad for you, Lord Chesterton, for in hearing of her actions with another engaged gentleman, when she herself was being courted by another makes me quite ashamed of the lady!"

Lord Chesterton nodded. "Indeed. And then to discover Lady Prudence thereafter... well, nothing could have prepared me for such joy."

Seeing the light that came into Lord Chesterton's eyes when he spoke of his wife and hearing the tenderness that came into his voice, Marie's own heart softened. That was what she had begun to feel for the Duke, was it not? That very same affection, albeit a good deal smaller than that which was, no doubt, in Lord Chesterton's heart. If only the Duke would listen to his friend! If only he would realize that there was that same happiness waiting for him – for them both! Martha pressed her hand and Marie looked over, seeing her friend's encouraging smile. This was already going well, she realized. Her husband had not yet quit the room nor refused to speak to his friend. Whether it brought the result she hoped for, Marie could not be sure but this, at the very least, was a good thing.

"Might I ask who Lady Prudence is?" In a low voice, the Duke put his question to Lord Chesterton. "You speak with such an evident fondness, it is clear to me that she means something to you."

"She does." Lord Chesterton smiled broadly and sat back. "She is my wife."

The Duchess beamed at Lord Chesterton, even though this was already known to her. Marie as well could not help but smile, seeing the joy on Lord Chesterton's face and knowing, without doubt, that he was truly happy.

"You... you are wed?" Seemingly incredulous, the Duke stared back at Lord Chesterton, who nodded. "And you are happy?"

"*More* than happy. We have only just returned from our honeymoon, truth be told, and I am already aching from being away from her!" Lord Chesterton chuckled softly as the Duke rubbed one hand over his eyes. "She is the most wonderful lady. She knows of the accident, she knows of the weakness of my leg but she cares nothing about that. All that matters to her is my heart. Every moment of my day is brighter because of her. Each second of my day is made complete because she is there with me. The accident did cause me a lot of pain, certainly, and I regret my foolishness in not listening to you, Wessex, but if it had not happened, then I am quite sure I would be utterly miserable now."

Marie clasped both hands to her heart, tears in her eyes. The way Lord Chesterton had spoken of his beloved wife made her both ache and joyous in equal measure. There was a pang in her own heart too, desperately hoping that she and the Duke might share even a *little* of what Lord Chesterton had expressed. Her throat aching as she fought to keep her tears at bay, she looked to the Duke and found him gazing straight back at her.

For what was the third time, silence spread through the room. Marie could not take her eyes from him, holding his gaze without hesitation and silently praying that somehow, in some way, he would be able to see a glimpse of the future they might share. How desperately she wanted him to forgive himself for what had happened, to realize that the burden of guilt was not one he had to leave clinging to his shoulders! Everything would be transformed in an instant, the moment he let it all go.

"I – I need to think." The Duke rose to his feet unexpectedly, turning to make to the door, only to stop and turn around again, coming back to Lord Chesterton. "Are you leaving today?"

"Tomorrow." Lord Chesterton did not try and prevent him from departing, seeming to understand the need that the Duke had to consider all that had been said. "I will be here to speak with you again, of course."

"Rupert, do you –"

"I need to be alone," he said, interrupting Marie as he threw out one hand toward her. "Without interruption."

Without another word, he walked from the room and closed the door tightly behind him, leaving them all sitting in silence.

Marie could not help the tears which fell like a storm on her cheeks. Her shoulders rounded and she began to sob, barely hearing Martha's comforting words. She did not know what she had expected but it certainly had not been that the Duke would simply leave them all! The harsh way he had spoken to her at the end, the way he had flung out one hand and interrupted her as she had spoken had injured her heart and, with nothing but pain rippling through her, Marie dissolved into sobs all over again.

Chapter Twenty-One

Rupert was utterly exhausted but still, he walked up and down the room, going from one end to the other over and over and over again. Everyone had, no doubt, already taken their leave and retired but he had been unable to even think about closing his eyes.

After the shock of the afternoon, he had made his way to the library rather than his study, though quite why he had gone there, he did not know. Sending a footman to tell his mother, Martha and Marie that he was present in the library and was not to be disturbed, he had whiled away hours simply pacing and thinking through all that had been said. Dinner had been sent to him and he had eaten some, but not a good deal. There was too much in his mind, too much in his thoughts for him to have any comfort from food.

Marie wrote to him. That thought returned, piercing his mind as it had done already. Marie was the one who had written to Lord Chesterton, she was the one who had brought him here. When he had first heard that, there had been nothing but anger burning through him and yet now, in the quiet and in the dark, he felt his anger shrivel to nothing. He could not hold anything against her, not when he realized *why* she had done such a thing.

As much as he felt he did not deserve it, as much as he felt himself ashamed of his past behavior towards her, Rupert knew in his heart that his wife cared for him. That was the reason she had written to Lord Chesterton, the reason that both Martha and his mother had encouraged her to do so. They all cared deeply for him and wanted him to return from his solitude and loneliness.

And yet still, he felt himself held back.

"I thought I would come to bid you goodnight."

Rupert started violently, clutching at his heart as Lord Chesterton came into the room. "Goodness."

"I startled you." Lord Chesterton grinned, then came a little further into the room. Picking up a candle, he began moving closer, bringing a fresh light into the dullness that had become Rupert's comfort. "I did not mean to do so."

Rupert watched his friend as he moved, seeing no sign of evident weakness in his gait. Relief began to wash over him as Lord Chesterton turned to look at him, a small smile on his face.

"I am glad to see you again, my friend."

"It is hard for me to hear you call me such a thing," Rupert admitted. "I have not felt like a friend to you for a long time."

"And I have never thought of you as anything else."

Closing his eyes, a knot formed in Rupert's throat. To hear Lord Chesterton speak to him in such a way was threatening everything he had set upon himself for the last few years. It felt as though it was all about to crumble and he was not sure what would be left if it did.

"Why did you not read my letters?"

Taking in a shaking breath, Rupert curled his hands tightly so he might control his emotions. "Because I could not bring myself to face you, even in written form. I was sure that you would be furious with me, that you would throw all the blame upon my shoulders and I could not bear that. I could not even look at myself in the mirror for many a month, such was my shame. I feared that, if there was more, I would not be able to survive."

Lord Chesterton let out a heavy sigh, shaking his head. Then, after a moment's pause, he strode across the room and poured two small measures of whiskey. Coming back over, he handed one to Rupert, then sat down opposite with a contented sigh.

"Do you recall that we used to do this a great deal?" he asked, as Rupert swirled his whiskey lightly, aware that he was still shaken by all that had been shared that day. "We used to sit and drink and laugh and talk about all manner of things."

"Indeed, I do remember." Rupert let himself smile, an action he was not particularly used to. "We were great friends."

"We *are* great friends still," Lord Chesterton told him. "I have not rejected you, Wessex. I never did. You have taken a burden that was not yours to carry."

Something inside Rupert broke apart. His whole being shook violently, forcing him to set the glass down. Dropping his head into his hands, he put his elbows onto his knees and dragged in air into his protesting lungs.

"There is nothing for me to forgive, nothing for me to set aside between us for you did nothing wrong," he heard Lord Chesterton say, each word like a thunderclap. "Let it go, Wessex. It was never yours to bear."

Still shaking violently, Rupert closed his eyes tightly, feeling a lump grow painfully in his throat. Heat pressed behind his eyes and he felt moisture on his cheeks. "I – I have lost so much," he managed to say, the words broken and his voice trembling. "I thought... I was sure that I had caused your life to near come to an end! And now... now I see it differently."

"My friend." Lord Chesterton set one hand on Rupert's shoulder as he lifted his head, wiping his eyes with the back of his hand. "There is nothing for you to cling to. Break free. Breathe freely and step into the life you are *meant* to have."

It was as though a chain which had been wrapped tightly around him was suddenly broken. Taking in one huge breath, Rupert threw his head back and gazed up at the dark ceiling, feeling as though his whole body was suddenly lighter.

"You have a beautiful wife, my friend," Lord Chesterton said, as Rupert dropped his head forward again, looking back at him. "She told me just how afraid she was of writing to me, terrified that the actions she had taken would break you apart but I assured her that she had done the right thing. I think now that I have proven myself correct, have I not?"

Rupert smiled, his heart warming him as he nodded. "Yes, I think so." A twinge of regret began to threaten his slow growing happiness but he dismissed it quickly. He was not about to let himself be bound with something new all over again. "It is as though a storm cloud has broken apart and finally sent down light into my world."

"Then I think you should tell her exactly that," Lord Chesterton smiled, holding out his glass for Rupert to chink. "To regained friendships."

Rupert tapped his glass lightly against Lord Chesterton's. "To the setting aside of the past – and to a new and wonderful future."

Epilogue

Looking at her reflection in the mirror, Marie's shoulders dropped. She looked wane, almost haggard, truth be told. There were blue smudges under her eyes, her skin pale with not even the smallest hint of color in her cheeks. Closing her eyes, she let out a long breath, wishing that she had slept the previous night. Every time she had closed her eyes, she had been assailed by worrying thoughts about the Duke, fearing that all she had done would fall upon her with a great and overwhelming weight. After he had quit the room, she had not seen him again for the rest of the evening, forcing her to retire to bed without the least idea as to what he was thinking, feeling or doing. That had been very difficult indeed, for even though both Martha and the Duchess had reassured her that they thought all would be well and had reminded her of how well the conversation had gone, Marie had not found any peace. Instead, she had lain in her bed, her eyes wide open as thought of the Duke had come to her over and over again. She had been afraid of what his reaction might be to seeing Lord Chesterton and yet now, even in knowing that they had spoken and that everything she had hoped for had been shared with the Duke, she had felt that fear all the same.

Just as she felt it now.

"Now, Your Grace," her lady's maid said, coming to brush her hair. "What shall we have this morning?"

"A chignon," Marie answered, wanting nothing more than the simplest of hairstyles. "Nothing more than that."

The maid nodded and set to work, though Marie caught the way she sent a slightly worried glance towards her now and again. She did not say anything in response, of course, for it would not be proper though at the very same time, she silently acknowledged that the staff, as a whole, would know all that Lord Chesterton and the Duke had spoken and would now be wondering what the outcome might be.

Just as she was.

"I thank you." With only the smallest of smiles, for she could not manage any more, Marie dismissed her maid and then rose, ready to go and break her fast. She had not wanted a breakfast tray this morning, thinking it would be best for her spirits to go and sit with the Dowager or Martha. They would soon be leaving, she remembered, tears pricking at the corners of her eyes as she walked to the dining room. Then she would be left alone with the Duke and as yet, she did not know whether that would be with any sort of happiness whatsoever.

"Your Grace?"

A footman approached her just before she entered the dining room. "Yes?"

"The Duke of Wessex would like you to speak with him."

A streak of dread raced up her spine, her breath twisting through her chest. "Of course. I thank you." She began to make for the study but the footman's voice stopped her.

"Pardon the interruption, Your Grace, but the Duke is not in his study nor his rooms."

A little confused, she turned. "Where is he?"

"The stables."

This made her worry redouble itself. "The stables," she repeated, thinking to herself that this was because of Lord Chesterton. "I thank you."

A trembling began to take a hold of her as she made her way out to the gardens and then to the stables. This was where the Duke and Lord Chesterton had argued that day, so many years ago. Why was he here? And why was he asking her to come?

Taking in a shaking breath, Marie closed her eyes as she paused at the threshold of the stables. Gripping tightly onto the door, she did her best to calm herself before she stepped inside. This was the moment; the moment she would learn what sort of future she was to have.

She could barely move.

"Marie?"

Hearing him speak her name, she opened her eyes and forced herself to move in through the door. "Rupert? Where are you?"

"Here." As she came into the stables, he emerged from behind one of the horses, brush in hand. He was clad only in his shirt and breeches, the button open at the neck. With flushed cheeks and a brightness in his eyes she had never seen before, he appeared to be almost entirely different to the gentleman she had seen even yesterday.

Dare she hope?

"There you are," he said, setting the brush down and coming out from the stall towards her. "I came out this morning to the stables to think and, well..." Glancing over his shoulder, he looked at the horse. "I thought this one needed a little grooming."

Marie blinked rapidly, a sudden heat hitting her core and beginning to spread out all through her.

"You are surprised to see me so."

"I am, yes," she said, struggling to get her voice above a whisper. "Why are you here?"

"I was thinking, as I said," he answered, catching her hand and sending another shock through her. "Lord Chesterton came to speak with me last evening, once you had all retired."

She managed to hold his gaze, her breathing rapid, her stomach tightening with a mixture of both fear and anticipation. What was it that had been said? And what had the Duke decided?

"I have held a burden to my chest for many years now," the Duke continued, looking straight down into her eyes. "But no more. It is gone, Marie. Cast down and thrown away. I do not bear it any longer."

Tears began to burn in her eyes as, for what was the first time in their marriage, the Duke smiled at her. With one hand captured by the Duke, the other hand settled against her heart, as if to contain the stunned surprise that captured her. Her breath caught in her throat as the smile grew, sending a fresh light into his expression and a new vivid intensity into his blue eyes. Heat began to climb up her chest and into her face as her heart began to ache, though it was not with pain or sorrow. Instead, it was with a new desire and a fresh affection, seeing now that all she felt for him no longer had to be contained, hidden away or pressed down.

She was free.

"Lord Chesterton made it very plain to me that he does not hold anything against me," the Duke told her, softly. "His letters said much the same, apparently, though you know that I had not read them, such was my guilt."

Managing to nod, a tear fell to Marie's cheek.

"But it is because of you and because of what you did in bringing Lord Chesterton here that I am able now to set that weight down," he continued, lifting his other hand to brush that tear away. "I wish that I had seen this sooner, wish that I had listened to my mother or to my sister long before this moment." The smile faded. "I cannot tell you how sorry I am that I did not."

She shook her head, yet more tears started falling. "There is nothing for you to apologise for, Wessex. You did not do anything wrong."

"Oh, but I did." Pressing her hand, he looked straight into her eyes. "I will hold onto my culpability in this, Marie. I had many people trying to tell me that I did not need to feel guilt over this accident and I did not listen to any of them. I was determined to hold onto it, quite sure that I was right to do so and that, in itself, was wrong. My sister cares deeply for me, my mother loves me and both of them tried, in their way, to reach me. But I pushed them away instead of giving their words any sort of consideration." Again, his hand lifted to brush away her tears but this time, it lingered, brushing down her cheek and then to the curve of her throat before his fingers brushed through a few wisps of hair at the back of her neck. "And then I rejected you, did I not?"

The tears fought their way forward again but Marie pushed them back, her body slowly beginning to come alive at his touch. "You did, yes. But I believe I pushed you back in my own way."

This made his lips quirk. "You certainly did, though you had every right to do so. All the same, we found a way through those difficulties and you were eager to keep walking along that same path with me. But I was not."

"You were afraid to let your heart feel anything."

"More than fear," he said, softly, moving a little closer as Marie's eyes went to the open neck of his shirt, then back up to his face, her breathing quickening. "I was terrified of what would happen should I let myself get close to you. I was terrified that I would injure you in the same way I injured Lord Chesterton. I may not have done so directly but I held myself responsible."

She pressed his hand. "But now, in seeing that you have no guilt there, you can finally let your heart free?"

"Yes, I can." His smile returned, joyous and beautiful. "And it is the most wonderful thing I think I have ever experienced. Marie, I cannot help but feel unworthy of you."

Her eyebrows lifted in surprise.

"You fought for this," he said, leaning his head down just a little. "You were the one who was determined to find a way to give us this happiness, risked all to find a way forward. Your determination, your hope and your care for me is more than I think I deserve."

Her throat constricted as love broke through, filling every part of her. Setting her free hand on his chest, just at his heart, Marie looked up into his eyes. "My dear Rupert, it is not because I care for you."

A flickering frown spoke of his confusion.

"It is because I am in love with you," she told him, softly. "Fool that I am, I fell in love with the Duke who wanted nothing more than solitude!"

Her teasing words made the Duke chuckle, sending another bolt of light and happiness straight through her. "It is because of you that this solitary Duke has returned to his family, to his home and to you," he said, releasing his hand but only so he could wrap it around her waist, pulling her close to him. "I do not think I shall ever deserve you, Marie, but I shall endeavour to prove you every day just how much I adore you."

Her eyes closed for a few seconds before the Duke's lips found hers. There was a softness there at first, a tentativeness from him that spoke of a new understanding, of all that he felt and shared in this one moment. As the kiss deepened, the sweetness of the moment bound them closer together, melting into each other's embrace, whispering promises about the joyous future that awaited them.

With her arms around the Duke's neck and his arms holding her tight, Marie smiled against his lips. Everything she had risked had been worth it. The night of worry, the tears, the concern... it had all led to this one, beautiful moment where she was being held by the gentleman she loved, knowing that he loved her in return.

The solitary Duke was no more, left now as nothing more than a shadow in the past. Instead, she would have Rupert, her husband, who would be by her side in the days, months and years to come, their hearts bound to each other, their love overflowing and a happiness surrounding their every moment together.

It was all she had ever wanted.

Extended Epilogue

"Where are you?"

Rupert chuckled to himself as he hid behind a tree, peeking out from behind it to see Marie and their eldest son, William, walking together hand in hand.

"There he is!" he heard Marie exclaim, as William let out a squeal of delight. "Go and find him!"

Rupert stayed where he was, only to let out a cry of feigned exasperation as his son found him, making William laugh aloud. Catching his son up in his arms, he whirled him around lightly, then held him tight, tickling him under his chin.

"You found me after all, then," he said, setting his son down and taking Marie in his arms instead. "I think I should always let you find me." He gently took her hand, offering her a soft kiss. She responded with a soft blush, and they shared a quiet moment of understanding. As they strolled through the garden, thoughts of the day's obligations drifted away, replaced by the simple pleasure of each other's company. Perhaps, he thought, he might find a way to have the nursemaid look after William and little Francis for a short while, so they could enjoy a peaceful walk together.

"I know exactly what you are thinking and the answer to that is no, we cannot," Marie laughed. "The nursemaid is having her afternoon off, as well you know and the maid is already watching Francis for when he wakes. Then he will be brought back to you and I so we might be together as a family. Besides," she said, with a twinkle in her eye, "I have a surprise for you."

"Oh?" Grinning at her, he turned to look at William who was busy chasing a butterfly. "Does it involve handing the children to another of the servants?"

She laughed and leaned into him. "No, it does not," she said, with a smile, her arm about his waist as they began to walk back towards the front of the house, William running to a waiting maid who had set out tea and cakes on the lawn for them all. "Come, it will be arriving very soon."

"Arriving?"

Marie said nothing, though the knowing smile on her lips made Rupert's heart warm all the more. She was the most beautiful, magnificent lady in the world, he thought, still hardly able to believe, some three years later, that she had ever consented to marry him. How much his world had changed because of her! How much joy and happiness was his, now that she belonged to him and he to her! Rupert dared not think about what his life might be like had she *not* married him. No doubt he would still be consumed with darkness and shadow and that thought terrified him.

"You are frowning."

"Only because I was thinking of what I would be like without you," he said, leaning over and pressing a kiss to her temple. "You know just how much I love you, do you not?"

She turned to look up at him, her eyes holding his. "You tell me so every day," she said, gently. "You *show* me how much you love me with all that you do. I am the fortunate one, Rupert. I am the one who has been blessed with so much and for that, I shall always be grateful."

"I am afraid I shall heartily disagree with you in that," he said, with a smile on his lips before he bent his head to kiss her again. "Be assured I always shall." This time, the kiss lingered, the world seeming to fade away. It was only when a distant sound caught his attention that he broke the kiss, his breathing a little ragged as he tried to make out what it was.

"They are here!" Marie's hand settled against his heart, a bright smile on her face. "My love, I have invited Lord and Lady Chesterton to stay for a few days. I thought… well, it has been some time since we have seen them all since I was in confinement and I know how much this friendship means to you."

Rupert's heart ricocheted in his chest, not looking at the approaching carriage but down into his wife's face. Her love for him touched everything in his world, made it all brighter, warmer and more beautiful. "You are my sole delight," he said, framing her face with his hands. "Thank you for this, Marie."

She smiled and kissed him again, just as the carriage drew near. With a broad smile on his face and joy in his heart, Rupert beckoned William closer and stood, one arm around his wife and his hand holding his son's tiny one. This was such a happy moment, he thought, as Lord Chesterton beamed at him from the carriage, all brought about by his wife.

"How delightful it is to see you all!" Lord Chesterton exclaimed, as the door was opened by the footman, though Lady Chesterton descended first, followed by their own two children both around William's age. "Thank you for the invitation, Marie."

"Yes, thank you," Lady Chesterton said, greeting Marie warmly and then smiling at Rupert. "We have missed being in your company! Although I must say, I am very eager indeed to meet the new arrival!"

Rupert watched with a smile as his wife took Lady Chesterton's arm and led her into the house, clearly more than ready to show off little Francis. William took Lord Chesterton's children, Stephen and Emilia, over to the maid with the cakes and within a matter of moments, all three children were sitting and eating contentedly. Rupert chuckled and set one hand on his friend's shoulder. "We are blessed, are we not?"

"Indeed we are," Lord Chesterton agreed, watching the children with a smile on his face. "I am truly delighted to be with you all again. It has been far too long, though we would not have intruded on Marie's confinement. I assume she is well recovered after the birth?"

Rupert nodded. "Indeed so, though I have told her I am contented with two children. I do not want her to endure any more pain."

"Just as I have said to Prudence," Lord Chesterton remarked, with a nod of understanding. "You clearly love her, my friend. I am very glad of that."

"I adore her," Rupert answered, his heart filled with happiness. "My life would not be the same without her, I know that for certain." Thinking of all she had given him, Rupert let out a long and contented sigh. "Indeed, I love her and she loves me. And that truly is the most wonderful thing."

THE END

Printed by Amazon Italia Logistica S.r.l.
Torrazza Piemonte (TO), Italy